I0846477

CHARMINGLY UNDIAGNOSED

Billie Longo

DEDICATION

Mom,
Thank you for being my biggest supporter. Although you weren't able to see the end, the excitement you held from the very beginning for this story has been my motivation to see this through. This one's for you.
I love you, always and forever.

TABLE OF CONTENTS

CHAPTER 1:
THE BREAKDOWN

"He's going to end up dead somewhere!" I shouted.

"Honey, no, he's not. He's going to be okay. Please calm down, Riley, please," Mom replied, trying her hardest to console me and grasp the situation at hand.

Mom always tried her best to fix what was wrong and comfort me, but this time she had no words to express or any idea where to start. She knew there was no overturning this one, no going back and I wanted to believe her. I wanted to calm down, but I couldn't. The tears kept falling until there were puddles on the floor, too much for the carpet to absorb. I lay there wanting it to end, wanting him to snap out of it and to come back home.

With a rasp in her voice that pierced through her chest like knives, Mom yelled, "Riley, Riley, are you okay? Are you okay? Riley! Riley, answer me!" Her cries of fear were such that I had never heard before, but Mom's desperate pleas for answers went unresponsive. I was on the floor so broken and afraid that I couldn't speak. I couldn't see. I couldn't feel. And I couldn't breathe.

"Liana, Liana, quick, go get her . . . go get her water! Quick! She's passing out! I'm calling an ambulance!" Mom exclaimed.

Liana, my best friend since we were ten years old, obeyed Mom's request and zoomed down the spiral staircase to raid the fridge in search of water in an attempt to help me gain my composure. Mom could do nothing but sit and watch in distress as her daughter, her youngest, her baby, lay there motionless on her bedroom floor; fighting to stay conscious.

The sirens came louder and louder, followed by feet stomping up the stairs and a bright light streaming in my eyes before a flash, trailed by darkness. It was just like right out of a movie, when real life becomes slow motion, when each blink of an eye feels like a lifetime. I felt hands lifting me up and placing me down on a stretch of white. I tried to imagine it as a cradle of snow—the cold peacefulness that a dark winter night brings. That has always been my comfort spot, my go-to when something was wrong. The tingling nose, the empty warmth of the chilled breeze on my cheeks and the touch of something so white, sheer, and forgiving always made me feel as if I were not alone. It was as if all my troubles would be answered and that someone or something was standing right beside me. But that wasn't the case. My imagination failed me, and I was faced with the reality that it was mid-August. I was overwhelmed with scorned temperatures and drenched in sweat. There was nothing calming or comforting about this moment. It was more like the gateway to hell opening and dragging me in against my will. My entire world crumbled to ashes, and no one could stop it—or maybe, no one cared. I let the weakness take over and fell into its gripping sleep.

When I awakened, it was as if I hadn't slept at all. My eyes weighed heavy, and my feet were weak. *This must surely be a dream*, I thought. *This can't be happening.* I rolled onto my side and fell back asleep, praying that this would go away. That it would all be okay. That we'd be a family again, but little did I know, that dream was gone.

Consumed with confusion, disgust, and rage, I couldn't fathom what was taking place. My thoughts began to race. *Why was he saying this? Where was all of this coming from? Sure, Mom had a temper at times and said things she shouldn't have, but don't we all?*

Mom gave me and Dillon everything we wanted and even more growing up. We were always fed, clothed, and well loved, which is why I don't understand why he did what he did. And the worst part, the most embarrassing of it all, was that everything was right there, posted on social media, for the world to view. I had to shut my phone off to stop all the messages and texts that I was receiving, asking if I was okay and what in the hell was going on. Mom and Dad were receiving phone call after phone call from frantic, concerned family members. Even Grandma, heartbroken over the phone, asking if what he was saying was true. Of course, it wasn't, but I'm sure many believed. After all, Dillon always wanted to be an actor growing up. It's what he did best. He put on a show for all to see; he was the center of attention and got the fame he desperately craved.

CHAPTER 2:
BACK TO THE BEGINNING

Dillon and I were always very close, despite the seven-year-age gap. We were always fooling around and making up games like one that we called "Memo," where I played his daughter, "Memo." In the game, Memo had a rare condition in which she was allergic to the carpet and would burn at its slightest touch. Also in the game, Dillon had a twin brother who was Memo's evil uncle, who would spontaneously appear to throw Memo onto the carpet. Within seconds, her evil uncle would transform back into her father, who would scoop her up and save her from the horror. Now that I think of it, maybe that was a sign right there that something was wrong with Dillon. Maybe the switching of characters from an evil uncle trying to cause harm, into a loving father trying to be a hero and save Memo from danger was his way of trying to express himself. Maybe he was trying to tell us he feels as if he were two different people in one body—or maybe I'm just over-analyzing now—considering the situation.

However, another strange thing growing up was that Dillon would tell me that he thought we were being followed or watched. He would say this because shortly after we created Memo, Disney's *Finding Nemo* came out and the names were too close for comfort in Dillon's eyes. A short while after that event, we would play a game where I was Brittney Spears and owned a restaurant, only to hear that the actual Brittney Spears was thinking of building a restaurant of her own. But at the time, I thought nothing of it. I was only a kid and brushed it off to be nothing more than a coincidence. Maybe Dillon honestly felt that someone was watching him his entire life and out to get him, but no one picked up on it.

Was that a sign? Was he trying to tell me something? Is this all my fault? No—no, I was only a kid. Could this have all been avoided if I paid more attention to detail? No. How would I have known? I was a kid. I was just a kid. But so was he. So was he . . .

I mean that would make sense. For the past few years Dillon's recurring paranoia that someone was watching us grew stronger. He would over-evaluate every unassuming car parked in front of our house as being a spy or some type of investigator. It wasn't out of the blue though for a car to pull up and park out front for a few hours a day. We live on a moderately busy street, with a middle school, strip mall, and nursing home. Dillon was incredibly persuasive and at times even had me considering the possibility that there were eyes lurking. Of course, I quickly came back to reality and rationalized the situation. The black SUV parked during the mornings must have belonged to a faculty staff member of the middle school. It would be parked in front of our house in the mornings before school would begin and be gone shortly after school let out in the afternoons, but only on school days. Dillon, of course, argued against my logic. He claimed that it was a private investigator keeping tabs on Mom since there was a lawsuit pending with a department store when she fell and injured herself a few years prior. The silver minivan parked during the late afternoon hours belonged to an individual who had a loved one in the nursing home on the left side of our house. The facility's parking lot often times became overcrowded, leaving visitors to park on the street. Even though I had witnessed the elderly man park, exit his minivan, and enter the building, Dillon was still adamant that there were cameras in the back of the vehicle. He took it as far as convincing Dad to make a forty-minute drive out to our house late one night solely to peak into the van's tinted windows to take a look.

Mom and Dad always managed to stay civil and co-parent the best that they could even though they divorced about fifteen years earlier when our younger brother,

Shane, died in a freak accident. He was only three. I don't remember much about Shane, considering I was barely six at the time, but I do remember that particular day as if it were yesterday. It was Saturday, April 13, 2002. I had been feeling ill for a few days, which ended up being strep throat and Mom needed to take me to the doctor. The only problem with this was that Dad couldn't take off of work, which left Dillon having to watch Shane for a few hours. This didn't go over well with Dillon since he was supposed to be going to a party for one of his friends and though Mom explained to him that she would gladly take him to the party after she got back, an argument occurred resulting in Dillon slamming the door behind us. He used such force that the wooden boards of the porch rattled under our feet.

An hour and a half later, Mom and I were on our way back from the doctor and picking up my antibiotics when her cell phone rang. Mom never answered the phone while driving but seeing that the call was from Dillon she made the exception and answered it on speaker phone. "Yeah Dillon? We'll be home in five," answered Mom.

"Shane fell," replied Dillon in a calm, almost impassive tone.

"Wha—what do you mean he fell?"

"He fell," repeated Dillon.

"We're around the corner. I'll see you in a minute," Mom uttered as Dillon hung up the phone.

"Argh! I swear, your brother," she mumbled as we turned into the driveway.

The second we walked into the house, Mom froze as if she were playing that children's game "Red light, Green light." I tried to pass by her when she stuck her arm out, blocking me, and pushed me out the door without even turning around. It's clear now that she was trying to shield me from seeing what was in front of her and trust me, I wish she had been successful. One of the only memories I have of my younger brother was of his lifeless body lying on the white tiled floor below the stairwell banister. I couldn't even make out which way he was facing, his head was covered in a crimson puddle; it was thick like if someone poured a gallon of red paint over his face. I wish it were only paint, like a sick joke. But it wasn't.

Mom knew that Shane was gone, yet she sat there in the puddle, cradling him in her arms. Dillon and I were told to wait outside. There were so many people there—policemen, paramedics, even firemen—and through all the sirens and chaos, I could still hear Mom yelling, crying, and begging them to keep trying. To help him. To do something. Dillon was questioned by a handful of police officers; his story never changed. He said Shane was playing on the stairs when he had to use the bathroom, taking his eyes off of Shane for a minute when he heard a bang. Dillon said he ran out of the bathroom the second he heard the noise and when he didn't see Shanc, he looked over the railing and saw him at the bottom. That's when he said he called Mom.

Shane left on a bed under a white tarp two hours later as Dad punched a hole in the wall when the door closed. I guess it was from frustration. Dad never really handled his emotions well; his hand turned purple instantaneously. Mom sat there, lifeless, with a white throw blanket around her shoulders that one of the paramedics put around her. That's when Dillon turned to our parents and asked them when he could go to the party.

I know that Mom and Dad assumed that Dillon was just in shock and hadn't processed fully what just took place, but was he? Was he in shock? Even I processed what had happened and he's seven years older than I. Am I the only one who thinks that that's an odd way for a thirteen-year-old to act? Why wasn't that a concern of theirs? Did they even question if his story was true? I mean the arguing and blame they placed on each other— it tore their marriage apart and once they split, they never spoke of it again. But was Dillon actually innocent? I mean, the way he appeared before me and Mom even left was erratic: the slamming doors, the stomping, the cursing under his breath and even his skin turning deep red all because he had to miss a few hours of a party. But was Dillon so angry to the point that he'd do something to Shane to get him out of his way so that he could go and be with his friends? Like, why didn't they push further on the fact that as Shane's body was being wheeled out, Dillon's only concern was still about going to that party? And why didn't anyone question him about him not dialing 911? He was thirteen . . . at that age one knows that sort of thing.

Okay, okay, back to the story here. Dad still remained active in our lives and if we were ever in need, he was there. Because of this, Dillon felt as if it were second nature to call and wake him up with the claims of there being cameras in the back of a van and a man spying on us. Those "cameras" ended up being nothing more than a wheelchair folded up in the back of the van and like I had told Dillon several times before, the vehicle belonged to an elderly man who was visiting someone in the nursing facility.

The suspicions of being followed didn't stop there; it continued with Dillon being convinced that strangers in the grocery store were following him and trying to pry information about his home situation. He claimed that a person struck up a conversation with him while in line at a local supermarket and began asking him questions about his house. He insisted that they apparently knew the layout of our kitchen and some other personal facts that I can't recall because I blew off that conversation, thinking it was just Dillon being Dillon . . . overthinking every small detail.

But why was he always suspicious of the people and things around him? Why was he so firm on believing that someone was watching our every move? Why would anyone have any interest in our lives at all? We were every-day, average people; there wasn't anything significant or special about us.

In school, Dillon was referred to as the class clown, always coming up with crazy skits, making students laugh, and teachers writing out detention slips. His antic went anywhere from going off script in school choir concerts, to jumping out of classroom closets that he'd hide in for hours, riding janitor carts down the hallways, breaking into the computer lab to set his face as the screen background on all of the computers and even shoving women's underwear into the bags of his male teachers for their wives to find later on. He had done it all. Students applauded him, they found humor in his acts, and teachers blatantly dreaded him. Suspension followed suspension. Dillon ironically seemed to expand on all of the attention and leveled up with each occurrence, trying to beat the one before as if it were a game. "What's next?" the administrators would say. Yet his conduct was always passed off as typical adolescent behavior.

But was it? Was this ordinary, or was this the beginnings of psychological suffering that flew under the radar?

Dillon continuously expressed that his actions and performances were nothing more than a distraction for his classmates, to give them something to laugh about. In elementary school Dillon was constantly teased about his weight, which ultimately led to a battle with eating disorders in high school. In an effort to deflect the pain from the name-calling and bullying, he found his escape in comedy and deviance, quickly rising to a reputation of tremendous popularity in school. Every student, teacher, and faculty staff knew who Dillon was and began each day waiting to see what stunt he would pull next.

Even years after Dillon had graduated teachers would question me if I was his sister and proceed to tell their experiences with him. Whether teachers had Dillon in class or not, they almost all had a story to tell. For instance, my chemistry teacher Mrs. Hays never personally had Dillon in her class, yet she would tell me how he would stand in the middle of the hallway outside of her classroom belting out her name at the top of his lungs. He went as far as making t-shirts and coffee mugs to sell in school that read

"I Love Melanie Hays," for which he later got suspended from school. Sometimes I would deny any relation to Dillon when asked, to avoid the embarrassment. In tenth grade, my psychology teacher said to me, "Oh, I know of your brother. Everyone *knows* of your brother." I slumped back into my chair, giving a faint smile, thinking to myself *I'm nothing like him.* I was tired of living in his shadow and having to prove to my teachers that, unlike Dillon, I was hardworking and respectful.

Dillon's actions were never violent in school or at home; aside from kicking a hole in the wall once, he never raised his hands to me or our parents. He would, however, yell and blurt out hurtful things when he was angry. But isn't that normal for a teenager? As Dillon grew older these outbursts of anger worsened and became more frequent. One minute he was cheerful and the next he would be screaming and cursing up a storm, most of the time with no cause in sight. Each passing year the recurrences of these eruptions became more common, and the words being said developed into a level of insanity like one would not believe.

CHAPTER 3:
DISCOVERY

"Riley, do me a favor," Mom expressed, exhaling, and taking a slight pause. "Go into his room and see if there's anything that gives away where he could be."

Although I thought that was a long shot, *what are the odds that he would leave something behind with his possible location*? I complied with Mom's wish and headed down the hallway to his bedroom door. I didn't think much of it and figured I wouldn't find anything except a few old receipts and cigarettes. Boy, was I wrong. Nothing could have prepared me for what I was about to uncover. I reached his door and before turning the brass knob I took a double take down the hallway, towards the window, to listen for any sounds of a car pulling into the drive way to make sure Dillon hadn't come home. Of course I knew he didn't; he had taken off two days prior, but I was overwhelmed with guilt knowing I was about to invade his personal space. I opened the door, flicked on the light, and stood there in pure disbelief.

"Oh, my God," I muttered under my breath.

"What?" yelled Mom, curious as to what it could be.

"What, what is it?" she asked again since I couldn't get myself to utter out a response in time.

"Just—just, his room," I replied, stumbling over my words.

I stood there in the doorway scanning his room from left to right, ceiling to floor. There were clothes, papers, cigarette boxes and trash piled throughout the room, stacked up three to four inches off of the floor. If I hadn't been home, I would have thought someone broke in or that a twister took hold of his room and flung anything and everything he had ever ate or owned. Unfortunately, it was obvious that none of the above had happened and that this was a buildup over the course of a few years. There were coffee mugs, plates, and silverware scattered on the floor, bedside night tables, and the television stand. Mugs and dishes that we had not seen in months, molded, and crusted. The gray, polished, wooden floor that my mother had put in for him as a birthday gift about three years before lay scratched and stained. The white wooden bedpost big enough for a king, now cracked and leaning to the side and his off-white, tannish-painted walls were now coated in a thick yellow tint from the nicotine as a result of endless smoking. It was so rotten that paint was beginning to chip off and hang from the depressed walls.

No wonder he's been sleeping on the couch for the past few months; it's absolutely appalling in here. He pleaded that it was due to feeling a level of paranormal activity at night and seeing figures at the end of his bed, but clearly it's because his room is a total shithole. I mean, who could live in here? What's that smell?

I gathered myself and dreadfully entered the room towards his bed, where another mountain full of trash was left. As I went to pick up a piece of crumbled-up loose-leaf paper, I spotted two silver keys with a vicious Pitbull design on them. It was his house keys resting on his bed, in plain sight.

What's this doing here? Didn't he say Uncle Jimmy cut it off his key chain and took it?

I picked the key up and took it to Mom. About three weeks before this whole ordeal took place, Dillon barged into Mom's bedroom accusing Uncle Jimmy of having cut the house key off of his keychain before leaving for work. Uncle Jimmy had been living with us for about three months at that point ever since he had been released from jail for violating his probation restrictions. He was actually a great help around the house; he would cut the grass and do slight handy work when needed, things which Dillon had never done. Not long after Uncle Jimmy moved in, Dillon began making comments to Mom about how he lives here for free and doesn't so much as help with the grocery bills or contribute anything towards utilities. This caused a massive fight between Mom and her brother in which Dillon listened in on from a window and sent a voice message simply stating "he'll be out soon" to someone through his phone. However, Mom and Uncle Jimmy resolved the conflict and made an agreement on rent.

Now that I think of it, Mom was perfectly happy with the original setup of having handy work done around the house for free, and never mentioned anything about help with the utilities or groceries until Dillon began to feed into her mind that he was mooching off of her and not contributing his fair share. Why was this any concern of Dillon's anyway? It's not like he had ever contributed anything to the household. Dillon wouldn't even mow the lawn for Mom which caused her to hire a landscaper for weekly cuts and better yet, he hadn't had a job since 2012. Five years! Doesn't that make him the moocher?

Anyway, back to the point; the very next day Dillon accused him of stealing his house key. He conveyed that it must have been cut off because he had glued it onto a leather holder that he crafted himself and showed Mom the remaining leather attached to the keychain where his key had been. It indeed looked as if it were cut off with a knife. Dillon then continued to bring up another incident that happened three months ago when Uncle Jimmy had first moved in. Dillon had taken Uncle Jimmy to the store to run some errands and when they returned, Dillon made a scene that his house key was missing. He went into such a panic that he convinced Mom to have the locks on the house changed, belting out someone must have taken it.

"Mommy, isn't it a bit strange that I have never lost a key before; then once he moves in, two have gone missing?" questioned Dillon.

"I don't trust him; he's trying to sneak around. I can feel it," Dillon added.

Mom, with no reason to not believe her son, texted Uncle Jimmy telling him he was no longer welcomed back into our house. She had made it clear to him from the very beginning that she didn't feel comfortable giving him a key to the house in case he fell back into old ways; she found it safer that way. She explained to her brother that she was aware he had been snatching Dillon's keys and would not put up with any of his games. Of course, he denied any doing with the missing keys, which Mom clearly paid no mind to it since he had a long track record of lying and stealing.

As if Mom telling her brother not to return wasn't enough for Dillon, he then ensued to text Uncle Jimmy to inform him that he came across his search history on Mom's computer for porno sites involving transgendered men and ads for prostitutes. Dillon referred to them as being his little secret. I never understood why Dillon felt the urge to bring his search history up and throw it in his face, when Uncle Jim's personal searching had nothing to do with a missing key nor when Dillon himself was innocent of clean web searches . . . like Dillon searching the internet on how to hire a hitman on Mom after one of their fights, which I'll explain more later on. But now it all makes sense. Dillon wanted to embarrass Uncle Jimmy to the point where he wouldn't respond back or try to prove to Mom that he didn't take Dillon's house key. Dillon wanted him out of the house for good and that's exactly what he got. He wasted no time in clearing out the guest room of Uncle Jim's belongings and leaving them in trash bags on the porch for him to retrieve after work. Now that I look back on it, Dillon waited by the windows and watched with a grin as Uncle Jimmy sluggishly picked up the plastic bags and headed towards the street. Mom's relationship with her brother, one of the only relatives that she had left, was now ruined, and all because of a phony missing key.

"Why would he have this?" Mom questioned, holding the key in her right hand, looking down in confusion.

"I don't know, Mom, but Dillon clearly set him up. The keys were never stolen; he had them the whole time," I replied, in a soft tone, just trying to make sense of it.

With my adrenaline pumping, I went back into Dillon's room, determined to find out more. There on his bed was an open pack of syringes. I picked them up and brought them to Mom and asked her why he would have her insulin needles in his room. However, Mom conveyed that she hadn't used syringes in years ever since the insulin pens had come out. In total shock, she claimed he must have been doing some type of drug, since those clearly weren't hers. Dillon had always told us how many of his friendships were destroyed from them being heroin addicts and pill poppers. He even swore on multiple occasions that he wanted nothing to do with them; we never once suspected that he was the user.

Then again, Dillon was a professional at directing suspicion away from him and onto everyone else. After finding the needles, I decided to put on my sneakers. I was barefoot and didn't want to risk stepping on anything in his room. On his bed, I started to find tiny plastic baggies scattered. I never knew much about drugs; I stayed away from them in high school and ended countless numbers of friendships with people who were users. So, being as oblivious as I was, I took these baggies as belonging to clothes that he had bought which must have come with a small bag of extra buttons attached to it. Pathetic, *right*?

I proceeded through his room and found envelopes addressed to Mom with her tax returns, bank statements, and all sorts of bills. I didn't understand why he would be hoarding her mail; what good did it do for him? I picked up the mail to move clutter and found a debit card broken in half with his name on it lying underneath the pile. That was odd, considering he hadn't had a job in years or any money for that matter. When I reached his dresser, I noticed a clear plastic bag with round yellow pills inside. I inspected them and noticed they had a "Q" on one side and a "100" on the other. I quickly looked up the pill online and discovered that they were Quetiapine Fumarate. Being a psychology major, I knew that these drugs were used to treat Bipolar Disorder, Schizophrenia, and other psychological ailments. He was never diagnosed with any mental disorder or illness, so I didn't comprehend why he would have these or how he would get them. But I finally began rethinking the other plastic bags I had found on his bed as being drug-related as well. I opened his jewelry box and found more clear plastic bags, along with some type of clear pipe, similar to a test-tube that I had used in science class, along with opened used syringes. In that moment I came to the realization that it was clear that Dillon had a problem. I continued rummaging through his drawers and found three more pipes, along with countless numbers of emptied clear baggies and dozens of needles.

After showing Mom what I had found, she instructed me to put it all back in his room, turn off the light, and close the door. We decided to stay out of there until Dad could come over and clear it out. I didn't want to end the search in case there was anything more serious we needed to know about; but I agreed that it was too dangerous for me to go through this horrific situation alone. God forbid I would step on an open needle.

I sent all the photos to Dad and explained what I had found. He too begged me to stay out of Dillon's room and explained that he would come over after work the next day to clear it out. This discovery was about to lead to a shattering chain of unfortunate events that no one ever saw coming.

The rest of that night Mom and I tried to glue together the pieces of everything I had found and form a storyline from past occasions, leading up to this wretched night. We tried desperately to put reason behind his actions.

What was he using? When did he start using? Why did he start using? Could this explain his short-tempered moods and his unprompted rages? Could this be why he slept all day, every day? Is this where the voices that he told me he heard in his head come from? Was this why he claimed to see figures in his room at night? Was he hallucinating? Was all this behavior due to his secret drug abuse? And why would he frame Uncle Jim? Why would he deliberately go through the trouble of cutting his key off his keychain and accusing him of taking it? None of this made sense. Why was all this happening?

CHAPTER 4:
DAMIEN'S INTRODUCTION

It was the end of July, a humid Friday night, around 11:46 p.m. I was just getting home from work at Fusion Freeze, a popular ice-cream and dessert shop. Exhausted from a busy night from training the new girl, I was unaware of my surroundings. I walked up the rocky driveway not paying mind to the fact that my dog wasn't barking as usual at the sound of the shuffling of the rocks from my approaching footsteps. I should have realized it was strange that he wasn't barking as soon as he heard my car pull into the driveway, but the only thing on my mind in that moment was getting inside, eating, and going to bed. As I entered the fogged-out glass door, Hershey wasn't there to greet me. Usually, he would be jumping up and down and running around from the excitement of my being home. I continued into the kitchen when I was startled by a strange man, who was about five-eight, in his mid-forties, with a thick build, feeding Hershey peanut butter—his favorite. Just as surprised as I was, the man quickly said hello in a very thick foreign accent which I could hardly understand.

"Oh Riley, how was work? This is my boyfriend, Damien!" Dillon said, eagerly, as he turned the corner into the kitchen from the bathroom.

"Oh, okay," I said, as I introduced myself to Damien. I was thrown completely off guard. Dillon had never mentioned a Damien before or that he even had a new boyfriend for that matter, and now there was a strange man standing in my kitchen, feeding my dog, and apparently staying the night. I continued my way towards the pantry to grab some cereal when Dillon made his way upstairs to his room, leaving Damien and me in the kitchen. Paying no mind to the awkward situation of this random man standing in the corner of my kitchen, I tried to pour myself a bowl of cereal as quickly as I could and head up to my room when Damien tried to strike up a conversation with me. I honestly had no idea what he was saying and must have said "What" six or seven times before just nodding my head as if I was agreeing with whatever he was saying. There were a few moments when he would stare at me for a few seconds after speaking. I guess he was waiting for a response, but I couldn't tell if what he was saying was even a question. Once Dillon came back into the kitchen, I excused myself and told them that I was going to bed.

I had an odd feeling about Damien that night. The way he held himself and the way his eyes would pierce through mine, something just didn't feel right.

The next morning while I was leaving for work I went into the kitchen to grab a water bottle and a quick snack. I was running late as usual. It was at this point that I noticed the office-room light which was located off to the side of the kitchen was glowing from underneath the door. This confused me because no one was ever awake so early. Dillon tended to sleep into the late afternoon hours; I just assumed that he forgot to shut off the light the night before. I walked back into the kitchen, opened the stainless-steel refrigerator, and grabbed a Poland Spring water bottle along with a red apple. As I closed the refrigerator door, I was startled by the reflection of Damien glooming in the doorway behind me. I gasped and dropped the apple, which bounced and rolled onto the floor. I turned around and let out a slight laugh apologizing for getting scared. I explained that I wasn't expecting anyone to be up this early and didn't notice that someone was behind me. Damien did not respond; instead, he stared back at me with no emotion on a stale face.

Feeling extremely uncomfortable, I hesitantly picked up the apple and excused myself for work, in which he slowly moved to the side so I could pass. I cautiously closed the front door, hand lingering on the knob begging me not to go as a knot began to form inside of my chest. My gut was trying to tell me something, but I couldn't figure out what. It was like being in school when you're trapped between two choices on an exam. They tell you to go with your first pick, your gut feeling. If only I had picked *A* instead of *B*. If only I had listened to my gut telling me that I was being tested and that I should stay.

Why was he in the office room? Nothing for him is even in there except Mom's computer which requires a password to access it and neither I nor Dillon knew it since it was recently changed after the incident with Uncle Jimmy. Was he trying to get on it? Why not just use Dillon's laptop, or his phone? Was he looking through our family photo albums that lined the shelves? What business would he even have with that? Where was Dillon? Why was Damien down there alone? How did he open the door so quietly that I didn't hear a sound? Why was he just glaring at me as if he was afraid I caught him doing something?

After work that day, I invited three of my work friends— Casey, Karen, and Alex—over to the house to go swimming. When they arrived, I introduced them to Damien who was sitting on the back porch by himself.

"This is my brother's uh, friend, Damien," I told them, stuttering over which word to use: boyfriend or friend. I was still bewildered by this new information that was only given to me the night before. The three of them greeted him as Damien mumbled an unfriendly hello under his breath. He didn't make any eye contact, but looked down at his phone, fidgeting with the buttons. He was obviously uncomfortable, like he didn't want anyone to make eye contact with him or get a good look at his face.

"What was that about?" asked Casey, referring to the interaction with Damien.

"Yeah, he seemed a little off," added Alex.

"I'm not sure. I just met him last night, but something about him is strange. Maybe he's just awkward meeting new people," I answered.

Three more days passed, and Damien was still at our house. My friend, Liana, stopped over with her puppy, so our dogs could have a play date while we swam in the pool.

She briefly met Damien who, for some reason, was cleaning out Mom's car while Dillon was doing yardwork, which ironically he had never done before.

Suddenly the extension cord attached to the leaf blower Dillon was using fell into the pool. He had two extension cords connected to each other as one wasn't long enough for the yard, and as he continued to pull further away the two ends that were connected inched closer and closer to the edge of the pool. Liana and I yelled out to him: "What the hell are you doing? You're gonna kill us!" Before acknowledging us, Dillon glanced over at Damien who shook his head and turned away from the situation. Dillon turned back towards the pool laughing and acting surprised. "Oh, I thought it was water proof," he responded. In that moment, I figured Dillon had simply made a mistake, but in retrospect of what I know now, it's obvious to conclude that Dillon wasn't being stupid. He was twenty-eight years old and knew damn well that an extension cord in water could have been deadly. Especially where the two ends connect!

Was he trying to get rid of me? Was he trying to make it look like an accident before he carried out the rest of his plan? Or was I just being paranoid?

Thirty minutes after Liana left, my phone buzzed and lit up with a text notification from her expressing a feeling she had about Dillon and his boyfriend.

Liana: I just feel they are up to something. - *Received at 4:32pm*

Liana: Bad. Really bad. - *Received at 4:33pm*

Riley: Yeah, me too. Can't pinpoint it but I get an off feeling about both of them and Damien's been here an entire WEEK now, Mom is so over it! - *Delivered at 4:36pm*

That night I went up to Mom's room with a piece of cake and sat on her bed. She asked me if Damien was still here which I told her he was. She rolled her eyes and in a sarcastic tone asked if he was living here now. I laughed and jokingly replied, "I think so!"

"What do you think of him?" she asked.

"I don't know. He seems nice, but I just get a strange feeling about him and I can't put my finger on exactly what it is," I responded.

"Well, what do you mean?"

"I don't know; he just seems weird or sketchy. Every time I turn a corner downstairs, he just happens to be standing there and he's always in the office. Do you think he's really just on the computer? Why doesn't he use his phone? Don't you think it's weird he walks around the house like it's his and makes breakfast, dinner, and bakes cakes every night?"

Mom and I continued to discuss our feelings about Damien and we both voiced that it was odd that everyone who had met him so far had gotten some type of strange vibe. We also discussed how Dillon hadn't been himself lately and had been caught in several lies since he had been around Damien. Dillon had been telling little white lies, such as claiming Damien had a job, when noticeably he did not, considering he'd been at our house for a week straight. When Mom pressed Dillon for more information about Damien's "job," Dillon was extremely vague and told her it's not that "type" of job—*whatever that means*. More lies of Dillon's include him telling Mom that Damien hadn't driven her car, yet I personally saw him behind the wheel on one occasion and Damien accidently out-right confessed another time to driving when they had run out of gas coming home from the mall a few days earlier, which leads to another story.

I was at work when I started receiving texts and calls from Dillon telling me he ran out of gas down the block. He asked if I could come get them or bring them gas which I told him I couldn't because I was at work. Dillon began cursing me out and becoming enraged because I wouldn't leave my job for his careless mistake. He even called Mom and became furious when she told him he would have to walk home to get the money from her and grab the gas container, walk to the gas station, then back to the car to fill it up. Dillon told Mom that he was driving and that he didn't notice the gas light was on. However, later that day, Damien told her he was the one driving and actually kept telling Dillon that they needed to stop for gas. He spilled that Dillon kept telling him not to stop and that Damien even had twenty dollars on him which caused confusion when Dillon insisted on walking back home to get money for gas. That's when Dillon kicked Damien under the table to signal him to stop talking.

If they had twenty dollars on them, why did Dillon act like he had no money? Why did he become so enraged when I wouldn't leave my job to bring them gas? Why did he go out of his way to walk thirty minutes back home to get money from Mom and thirty minutes back to the car to fill it up?

Anyhow, back to the main story. There were a few more scattered lies here and there—too many to remember but nothing too outrageous, just enough to have us double-thinking everything that he said.

CHAPTER 5:
THE FELON

I was at work at Fusion Freeze the next day, filling the ice-cream machines, ringing up customers, frosting cakes, and the usual day-to-day tasks that come along with working in a dessert shop. I was eager to leave so I could begin packing. Mom and I were going to Las Vegas the next morning for three days. Mom had received a three-night complimentary stay at MGM Grand Hotel and Casino. She was always receiving some type of offer since she's a gambler. Not one of those addicted throw-away-your-life-savings' gamblers, but the kind that is wise and knows which machines to hit and when to stop. I mean, that's just what I've heard throughout my life from family members. I had never actually witnessed it since I had just turned twenty-one.

In the middle of bagging up a grouchy customer's cake, the screen of my smart phone lit up and through the corner of my eye, I noticed the green flashing notification at the top left corner, which alerted me that I had received a text message. I glanced down, quickly getting a glimpse of the text and saw that it was from Mom. "Well, you were right" was all I could make out from the message before the screen went black and I was abruptly interrupted by the aggressive shuffling of a paper bag and mumbling from the customer I was assisting:

"Where are the spoons? You kids never do shit right these days; you're all self-centered and think an old guy like me has the time to come back here out of my way when I get home and have nothing to eat the damn thing with, you—"

"Sir, I put two spoons in the bottom of the bag, but I can get you more if you'd like," I uttered in.

"No you didn't; look, look; I'm all in this damn bag—there's nothing here!"

Just then the paper bag tore from the force of the man attempting to stretch it out to show me how there were "no" spoons as two plastic spoons fell out from the rip and onto the counter.

"You see what you did? Now you tore my bag!"

Are you kidding me? I didn't even TOUCH your bag. You had your beefy hands flapping through it like you were having a seizure or something; of course, it's going to rip. It's not like it's a rubber band. It's paper; what did you think was going to happen? Is all this really necessary over two fucking plastic spoons?

I would have been fired long ago if I had let my thoughts dictate what I said. Instead, I was forced to put on the standard customer service voice. "I'm sorry about that; let me give you a new bag and a few extra spoons. Hope you have a great day!"

I flashed a smile and directed my attention towards the new customers that were filling the store. I tried to assist them as swiftly as possible to get them out of the store so I could finish reading the message from Mom. I wanted—no, I needed—to know what I was right about. She never admits when someone else is right and I couldn't bear the wait any longer to see what it was about.

The store emptied and I was finally free to look at my phone. Without further delay, I picked it up, unlocked the screen and opened the message.

Mom: Well, you were right about Damien. Multiple arrests, identity theft, drug, assault and robbery charges. WAS ON CALIFORNIA'S MOST WANTED LIST! He took off to Puebla, Mexico and was extradited back here in 2010. Served 7 years in prison, guessing he recently only got out. Also goes by several different names. - *Received at 12:26pm*

I couldn't believe what I had just read. I asked her what she was going to do and if she thought Dillon knew this information already. She wasn't sure if Dillon knew or not, but she didn't want to confront him about this issue yet. She wasn't certain how he would react, and in all honesty, I don't think she had fully processed the material that she just uncovered.

It seems like my parents were always walking on eggshells around Dillon, trying to appease him and not say anything that could possibly set off one of his mood rampages. We were never really sure though what would set him off or when one of these rages would strike. One minute he was down to earth and respectful; then the next, his baby blue eyes were engulfed in red flames, destroying anything in his path. To be honest, we were all fearful of him to an extent. Not *lock-your-doors-when-you-sleep* kind of fear, but more of a *stay-clear-from-him-when-he's-in-a-mood* kind of fear. He used to drive me to school in the mornings, when it wasn't cool to take the bus anymore in high school, and I dreaded waking him up.

I would stand in front of his bedroom door, for what seemed to be hours on end, with my heart pounding in slow motion and a pit clenching my stomach, trying to build up the courage to knock and call out his name. Maybe I should have taken the bus instead of dealing with the huffing and puffing, heavy stomping and silence. Not a word would be spoken from our house to the school, and I wouldn't even move much. I would stay still as a statue and silent as a mute, afraid of being a trigger to set him off.

Why did we always avoid it? Why wasn't it talked about? Why didn't Mom and Dad confront him head-on instead of dodging it as being normal behavior?

But back to what I was saying. Mom decided that she wasn't going to mention anything to Dillon yet, until we came back from our little get away. Mom wanted it to be as stress-free and enjoyable as possible and it bought her more time to think about how exactly she was going to approach the situation. We were only going to be away for three nights. What could possibly go wrong in three nights?

Within a few minutes of receiving the message from Mom, I spotted Mom's forest green Explorer entering the parking lot of my job. I knew in an instant it wasn't Mom; she's disabled and unable to drive anymore. It clearly had to be Dillon. As the doors opened, I realized that Damien was the one driving and Dillon was the passenger. *Gosh, Mom would not be pleased over that one, that's for sure. God forbid he got into an accident, or didn't have a driver's license and got pulled over. The car would be impounded, the fines, the liability, it would just be a disaster.* I immediately shot Mom a text asking her if she gave the okay for Damien to drive her car, which I highly doubted.

My heart raced and my chest clenched skin tight as they approached the door to my job. I had to act like I knew nothing was wrong, like I didn't know that Damien was a convicted felon. Dillon acted like he was on cloud nine, living the high life. He walked with a bounce in his step, as if a weight had been lifted from his shoulders while Damien sauntered behind, tensed and anxious. It was an odd combination if you ask me. After filling their cups to the max with candy from the candy bar, they placed their containers onto the counter to be weighed.

"*$21.69,*" I stuttered.

Dillon reached into the front pocket of his jeans and pulled out a stack of cash. Dillon had not worked or held a job for nearly six years, making it clear that Mom must have given him money. But why wouldn't she have told me that she was sending him out to get sweets? Maybe she didn't even know that he was here, because usually she'd text me and ask for a milkshake or some German chocolate fudge cake that she loved. Dillon didn't even fill a cup of candy for her, not even a few pieces. Nothing.

While completing the transaction, chills ran down my spine from the strength of Damien's glare seeping into my skin. He didn't say a single word the entire time he was in the store, just a slight head nod when I handed them the covers for their cups as they turned and headed for the door. I stepped down from the step behind the counter and watched as they walked into the liquor store next to Fusion Freeze. After making sure the coast was clear, I snatched my cell phone off of the counter and headed into the back to inform Mom of the awkward encounter.

Mom: How do you know he was driving? - *Received at 1:16pm*
Riley: Was just in store. Saw him pull into parking lot; did you give Dillon money? - *Delivered at 1:45pm*
Riley: They went into liquor store after too - *Delivered at 1:46 pm*
Mom: What the hell. I sent him to store for Sloppy Joe mix. Tired of this shit - *Received at 1:51 pm*

This wasn't the first time Dillon had done something like this. For a little over a year now, every time Mom would send him out to the store for something, he would come back with everything and anything except for what he was sent to the store for and rarely ever had any change left over. He'd constantly give excuses that he forgot what he went for, or that he couldn't find what Mom wanted. Even grocery shopping was becoming a mystery. Dillon would only return with two or three bags of groceries, but the bill would come out to be close to three hundred dollars. The math didn't add up and each time Mom asked for a receipt Dillon would claim that either they didn't give him one, or that he couldn't find it. There was always some kind of excuse or reason why he couldn't show proof of what he bought, yet Mom had never questioned him further on the situation because she didn't want to accuse her son of something that extreme. Because . . . who would steal from their mother—*right?*

Mom was undoubtedly furious and when Dillon got home, she went downstairs to confront him when she saw Damien standing over the stove cooking. It surely did not look like Sloppy Joes, so she asked Dillon what they were making. Dillon told her they were cooking steak and instantly Mom's eyes expanded, and her eyebrows dove in. She had the *Mom* look—that simple stare that alerts every kid that they just messed up. Dillon asked her what was wrong, and she told him that he knew that I didn't eat steak, that she sent him to the store strictly for Sloppy Joes. She was getting fed up with him going to the store and coming back with everything except what she sent him to the store for and blowing through her money like it was candy. Mom then asked for her change back, becoming even more tense when Dillon told her there wasn't any.

Letting out an aggravated "huff," Mom went straight into confronting Dillon about Damien driving her car, which Dillon immediately denied. Mom and Dillon had a few exchanges, ultimately ending with Dillon flinging a clear glass salad dish across the kitchen, which had belonged to my grandmother. Shards of glass exploded against the wall, sending pieces in all directions. My Chocolate Labrador, Hershey, took cover from the impact by hiding underneath the table, peaking out with his sad brown eyes, waiting for confirmation from Mom that it was safe to come out. He was always terrified of loud sounds and yelling and often took cover under anything that would provide sanctuary. Dillon stormed outside, slamming the door, and aggressively speeding off, leaving Damien alone in the kitchen to clean up the mess.

About an hour had passed when Mom received a text from Dillon saying that he loved her, acting as if that argument earlier never took place. I watched Mom struggle over a response, watching her type out replies only to backspace and start again. She did this about three or four times before placing her phone down, ultimately deciding against entertaining his mood switch. She did what she had grown accustomed to, what she had done time and time again—she ignored the behavior, the mood change, and situation, praying that it would it go away.

CHAPTER 6:
VEGAS RETURN

Our three-night Las Vegas stay turned into a four-night stay due to a migraine I had the morning we were supposed to check out. Well, at least, that's what Mom and I told Dillon. We were having such a great time and weren't in any rush to return home. It was refreshing to take a break from Dillon, his constant lies and unpleasant behavior. It was like calling out of work for a sick day when in reality you're going to a party. We were really pulling one over on him . . . well, so we thought.

The next day Mom sent Dillon a text to inform him that we were finally on our way home which he responded that he had just left to spend the night at Damien's in Compton, California. Compton is a heavily populated town about thirty-five minutes away from where we lived in Los Angeles and profoundly known as having one of the highest crime rates in America; it's certainly not a place people flock to. Damien living in Compton didn't come as a surprise to us; it made sense after discovering his history and background. It was like another piece to a puzzle, like the perfect setting for a mystery novel. Mom and I were relieved though that he wasn't going to be home that night. We were eager to have an extra day of being stress free. Well, the joke was on us, that's for sure.

After a four-hour car ride that turned into six due to traffic and bathroom stops, we finally arrived home. I helped Mom from the car, along the gravel driveway, up the wooden, tree-bark brown stairs of the porch, and into the door. But when we entered, we were met with silence. I mean Hershey was barking up a storm and jumping excitedly to greet us, but other than that it was silent. It was a strange, empty silence like if you were in an old, abandoned building where belongings were left behind, yet you could still feel a presence. It wasn't an unnerving, eerie presence, but a disquieting, something-is-off feeling.

Mom made her way to the stair lift and plopped down to take off her shoes. Hershey began whining and nudging at my leg, which meant he had to relieve himself outside. I began walking down the narrow hallway, surrounded by pale walls, towards the back door to let him out when an unsettling sight struck me. There were dishes piled in the sink, half-emptied glasses scattered about the table, juice splatter on the ceiling as if someone used a blender without its cover—only we didn't have a blender—and a few dust-layered boxes resting on the counters.

That's odd; since when does Dillon leave the kitchen a mess? He's always cleaning it and getting frustrated if I leave a dish in the sink. And why did he bring boxes up from the basement? Mom asked him to organize it, not spread the mess throughout the house. Ha, she's going to flip on him. I can't wait to make some popcorn and grab a front row seat for this one.

"Riley, come here," Mom called out in a confused tone.

"Yeah, one sec. I'm waiting for Hershey to come in," I answered.

After Hershey trotted back in with a wagging tail and lifted ears, waiting for the treat he gets every time he comes back in, Mom yelled out for me once again. She was still seated on the chair lift directly across from the living room entrance with a dazed and muddled look, pointing towards the living room with squinting eyes.

"What is that—all that stuff in there?" she asked.

The room was decorated completely different than how we left it when we went to Las Vegas. Not as drastic as that time when Mom and I returned from Florida to find every wall in the kitchen covered in chalkboard paint. Or the time Dillon secretly painted the brick floor in the sunroom with the orange-brown color used for the living room walls. Or the time Mom and I went out for dinner only to return home to find the wallpaper in the bathroom completely torn off the walls because Dillon had felt the need to repaint. The outcome of that episode was that the walls remained bare for eight months because Dillon was no longer in the "mood" to paint by the time he had torn off the wallpaper. Mom ended up hiring a company to paint and finish the mess that Dillon had started. If she hadn't done that, the bathroom probably would have still been bare to this day. And of course, this time wasn't as painful and heartbreaking as the time Mom took me and a friend overnight to Knott's Soak City, a waterpark in Buena Park, California. It was just an overnight trip when Dillon was sixteen and he opted to stay home instead of joining us. When we came back home, we were met with all of Shane's belongings from his room thrown out onto the curb. Dillon preached and took it upon himself that three years was long enough to preserve his things and that Mom needed to get over mourning someone who "wasn't coming back." That one really took a hit on her. Dillon eventually converted Shane's Thomas the Tank Engine room into the guest room. I don't think Mom ever stepped foot into that room again, now that I think of it.

This time, however, the shelves were covered with glass bottles that he had painted. He recently picked up arts and crafts as a new hobby, and he was good at it. He really was. But my video games and DVDs that were on the shelves were tossed along the floor as if a raccoon attacked a garbage bag that was left outside, and his painted bottles were in their place. The coffee table in the center of the room that had belonged to my grandmother was covered in paint brushes, scraps of material, astrology books, and trash. A dozen of Mom's Matryoshka dolls—you know those wooden Russian dolls that twist open in the middle to reveal a smaller doll which twists open to reveal an even smaller one, and a smaller one and a . . . well, you get the point. Anyway, many of these dolls were also my grandmother's and were packed away in their original boxes, but now they were arranged on the mantel of the brick fireplace like a scene you would expect to see in a horror film about possessed dolls, along with several other antiques belonging passed family members.

"Oh, my God, what in the hell is he doing? I keep telling him that we need to get this fucking house in order! All he keeps doing is destroying this damn house. I can't do it anymore! He has no respect for anything," Mom continued, rambling on out of frustration.

I reassured her that I would take care of the newly decorated living-room, place everything in their respective boxes, stack them in the basement where they belonged, and have the living-room looking like it was before we left. We had just had an amazing time, won a few hundred bucks on the slot machines, walked the famous Vegas Strip which had shops, restaurants, and carnival rides, and treated ourselves to a few alcoholic beverages thrown in here and there. I didn't want her stressing after such a peaceful get-away. I told her to go upstairs to her room and relax, because out of sight, out of mind, *right*?

I began boxing up the Matryoshka dolls, picking up my video games and DVDS off of the wooden panel floor, and picking up trash left behind when I heard the upstairs bathroom door creek open, followed by a pause, and Mom ranting to herself: "What the hell is this?"

Oh boy, I thought. I placed the last DVD on the shelf and headed up the stairs to see what else Dillon had done. It was kind of an odd feeling walking up the stairs. The carpet under my feet was soft and comforting, hugging each foot with each step. But I knew underneath there was a rough, wooden stairway and that the carpet was only masking its true identity beneath something pure and deceiving. Now that I think of it, the stairway is just like Dillon. At first glance he seems like a well-rounded, charming, young man. But underneath his smooth tan skin, blonde hair, and light grin lurked a wooden stairwell. He was rough, manipulative, and misleading.

As I reached the top of the stairs and continued towards the bathroom door, I asked Mom what was wrong.

There she was, standing over the sink staring in defeat at a chain and the back of the toilet that was resting in it.

"What is that?" I asked.

"They're parts belonging to the toilet," Mom answered.

I couldn't understand why he would take apart the toilet and just leave bits and pieces of it in the sink. I certainly didn't know how to fix it or where the pieces even went for that matter. Mom exhaled loudly and returned to her room where she fell onto her bed, exhausted and drained of all energy. She regretfully lifted her phone and sent a text message to Dillon asking what the hell had happened here.

Dillon: What do you mean? - *Received at 8:18 pm*

Mom: The house is a mess; what happened to the toilet and why did you bring all that stuff up from the basement and put it out in the living-room? Riley's games were left all over the floor. - *Delivered at 8:24pm*

Dillon: What do you mean it's a mess? Toilet wouldn't flush so I tried to fix it and got distracted, I'll fix it when I come home. - *Received at 8:33pm*

After a few minutes of trying to get Mom to relax, I went into my room to unpack my suitcase. As I entered, I got a strange sense. Things were moved. They weren't in the same spot that I left them. I'm extremely specific about where things are placed. I guess you can say I have a splash of OCD—the slightest movement of something and I'll pick up on it. But things were without a doubt moved.

I took a second to look around to examine and noticed my sky-blue water speakers, that splash colorful water streams to the beat of whatever song is playing, were unplugged and in the center of my dresser. Dad had gotten them for me as a Christmas gift about four years before and they had always remained in the same spot, one on the left edge of my dresser and the other on the right edge to balance out the sound. And now they were unplugged and moved. I grabbed them furiously and stormed into

Mom's room, adrenaline pumping. "He fucking went through my room!" I yelled.

Mom's expression went stale, and her mouth slowly opened as her eyes grew wider. It was as if she just grew to the realization something horrible was about to take place, that her son had stepped over the line of no return.

Before Mom and I left for Las Vegas, she had asked me to take the envelopes of cash that she had in the filing cabinet in her closet and hide them somewhere in my room. She felt uneasy about Damien being in the house after learning about his criminal history and quite frankly, Dillon's recent behavior had us all on our toes, not trusting what he would do.

I took the four envelopes, totaling in forty thousand dollars, zipped them in my backpack and threw it into the back of my walk-in closet that had stacks of clothes piled up to my knees. In order to get to the back of the closet, one would have to climb on top of the mess and make their way through. I figured the bag was safe back there. I mean, who would waste their time rummaging through such a mess? I really should have cleaned it up a bit. I got lazy, I'll admit, but that's not the point.

Mom, pale and motionless, asked me to go check the money. I immediately went back into my room and opened my closet door. My unzipped backpack was lying in the middle of the clothes pile. I grabbed it and with the same pale, emotionless expression, brought the backpack to her to show her that it was open.

I emptied out the bag on her bed and all four envelopes were there. I let out a sigh of relief, but she stuttered and told me to count them. Each envelope originally had $10,000 dollars in it, I know it's crazy to keep that kind of cash in the house, but Mom had to keep most of her money out of the bank so that I would be able to get financial aid to attend college. She was disabled, unable to work, and had no income. The money that she was living on was left to her by my grandparents after their passing. It wasn't like she wanted to cheat the system. She had to do what she had to do to send her child to school though.

I counted the first envelope, and it came to $8,200. In disbelief, she had me count it a second time, then a third and fourth time. Each time yielded the same amount, $8,200. I moved onto the second envelope and counted $9,900, the third $9,300 and the fourth envelope had $7,600. $5,000 dollars was missing. Tears began running down her face; she leaned forward and yelled into her pillow. She was totally defeated and without hope.

Mom gathered her composure and sent Dillon another text:

Damien is no longer welcomed in this house and I think you should leave as well. I don't like who you are becoming. You're turning into nothing but a liar. Our rooms have been gone through and there are things missing, which I'm telling you now better be returned by tomorrow. - *Delivered at 10:16pm*
Dillon: Oh yeah, like what? - *Received at 10:18pm*

Like what? Is that really his response to being confronted about stealing? If I was being accused of stealing things, I would have immediately called her up and asked her what she was talking about, not asking what was missing. It's like he doesn't want to admit to something in case that wasn't what she was referring to. Like he wanted to know how much she knew before saying anything.

Dillon: I really hope you aren't trying to look for things to blame on Damien now that you know his history, and no one went into Riley's room. Was just in there to give her lizard water like she asked - *Received at 10:19pm*
Mom: Like money. And no, Dillon, her room was gone through. Her speakers were moved, things are missing. - *Delivered at 10:27pm*
Dillon: If you're talking about your change jar I moved it behind your wall when I was cleaning your room. You're welcome - *Received at 10:49pm*

Mom and I stared blankly at each other, shocked at his responses. Mom's room definitely was not cleaned; there were boxes scattered throughout, a step ladder had been placed below the ceiling entrance to the attic, and dust coated the top of her dresser from boxes being taken down. He clearly wasn't taking the situation seriously and thought he could manipulate us into thinking it was our own imagination by lying and denying.

CHAPTER 7:
SUSPICIONS

It was a quiet morning; we were tiptoeing around what had happened the night before. It was obvious Mom was at a loss for words and not quite sure what to do. She was in denial that her son would stoop so low as to do what he did and steal thousands right from under her. I wasn't too sure what to do either. I didn't want to believe that my brother would commit such a selfish act. But then again, it was evident that something eerie had been building inside of him for the past few weeks. He hadn't seemed the same ever since Damien came into his life.

It was just shy of twelve p.m. when keys jingling at the front door grabbed Hershey's attention, causing him to growl at whoever was there. Of course I knew it was Dillon, but it was odd that Hershey didn't realize. He never growls at any of us—usually an excited bark, but never a growl. It was as if he didn't pick up on his scent or recognize him like he normally does when one of us returns home. I didn't think too much of at that moment, but Hershey's growls were a warning that this wasn't the Dillon that we knew.

I didn't go down to greet him, instead I stayed in my room, partly due to not knowing what to say or how to react to him, but also because I wasn't sure which "Dillon" was walking through the door. Was it the charming, bubbly Dillon, or the rampage, out-for-blood Dillon? Jolly footsteps bounced up the stairs and I held my breath as he approached my room.

"Hi, Riley," he said as he skipped past my door towards Mom's room.

Dillon enthusiastically knocked on Mom's door and entered before she had the chance to respond. I quietly moved closer to my doorway to hear what was happening, expecting World War III.

"Hi, Mommy, do you want a cup of tea?" Dillon asked, as if nothing had happened.

"Sure . . ." Mom replied, after taking a long pause.

Once Dillon skipped back downstairs and into the kitchen, I headed into Mom's room. I stood in the doorway with a nervous smile painted on my face in complete shock at what to say.

"What . . . the hell . . . is wrong with him?" Mom asked.

Without knowing what to say, I shook my head and let out a nervous giggle as I sat on her bed.

Dillon returned and placed the mug down on the seat of Mom's walker and bounced back out of the room.

"What is he, a fucking rabbit?" asked Mom.

"Eh, I was thinking Tigger," I replied. "But seriously, I wouldn't drink that. I don't trust him."

"Neither do I," Mom responded.

It's terrible that the thought of Dillon possibly doing something to her drink even crossed our minds, but to drink it wasn't worth the risk. About a year ago, Dillon began "joking" about poisoning Mom and posting on social media that he puts "special" ingredients in her meals. One post contained a video of an odd-looking meatloaf in the oven with Dillon singing a tune he made up of how he created a "special" meatloaf. He accompanied the post with a caption that read "She won't know what hit her" with a winking face emoji. I sent Mom the link to the post to warn her since I was away at college and not home to personally protect her. Though we assumed Dillon was in fact only joking, the sound in his voice gave the both of us an uneasy feeling.

Our suspicions rose even more when he refused to take her to the emergency room on one specific night. Mom was having excruciating stomach pains, to the point where she asked to go to the hospital. Anyone who knows Mom knows how stubborn she is and how she never seeks medical attention unless absolutely necessary. It was impossible for me to drive her as I just had knee surgery two weeks before, putting me on crutches and pain meds. Instead, she asked Dillon, but he refused. She asked him several times and with each one, his response was "No", leading me to call an ambulance since Dillon refused to do that as well. Mom crawled from her room to the top of the stairs where she waited for the paramedics to arrive. Dillon wouldn't even assist her down the stairs. He lingered there watching her struggle with somewhat of an accomplished look in his eyes. Thankfully, Liana came over right away and took me to the hospital to see her because Dillon was refusing to even take me, claiming he didn't feel like going.

Why was he acting like this? Why did he just stand there while Mom was on the floor practically screaming in pain, refusing to take her to the hospital? Why did he watch as she struggled to crawl to the stairs? What was this coldness that overtook him?

I'll never forget the look of fear and helplessness on Mom's face in the emergency room when she asked me if I thought Dillon had actually poisoned her. I wanted so badly to reassure her that he wouldn't do something like that, but what else was I supposed to think considering the way that he was acting? What other assumption could we make when he seemed to enjoy watching his mother struggle on the floor?

That night when Liana and I returned home, we found Dillon dancing by himself in the kitchen. He was in his bath robe with a feather behind his ear blasting Brittney Spears, without a care in the world about Mom.

"Oh hi! How's Mommy? I'm going to go sleep over tomorrow," sang Dillon.

Sleep over? Did he just say he's going to go sleep over like it's some kind of party? Four hours ago, he was standing over her ignoring her pleas for help and now he wants to go sleep over? What the hell is going on?

"Um, they're running tests," I replied, as Liana and I exchanged looks of confusion.

Though Mom was released from the hospital a week later, the doctors weren't exactly sure what was wrong with her, but the thought of Dillon being involved in some way has always lingered in the back of my mind. That explains why I was on high alert when he brought her up tea and acted like he had no awareness of the accusations of his stealing while we were away.

Not sure how to handle the situation, I texted Dad to fill him in on the missing money and the way Dillon had been acting ever since he had met Damien. Flabbergasted, Dad texted Dillon asking him if he had stolen money from Mom. Of course, Dillon denied it and sent a text to Mom telling her that he was leaving because he did not like being accused of things that he hadn't done.

Mom told him that he was free to do whatever he wanted to do, with the exception that the car was to remain in the driveway and that he was not to leave with anything that he hadn't personally paid for, which amounted to nothing. Dillon stormed up the stairs and slammed the guest room door shut, which is where he had been staying ever since the whole key ordeal with Uncle Jimmy took place. Obviously this was because his room was totally unlivable, but we just didn't know that at the time. He told us that it was due to hearing, feeling, and seeing spirits over his bed during the night which no red flags were ever raised by those comments, but now that I think of it, it was probably a sign of his paranoia and delusions.

CHAPTER 8:
THE PHONE CALL

Because of the chaos that took place earlier that day, we were all staying in our rooms doing our own thing, staying clear of one another. It was basically an average night of walking on eggshells with Dillon, too anxious to leave our rooms and if we did, we made damn sure to make it unknown to him. It wasn't that we feared Dillon physically doing harm to one of us, but more so just nervous to tick him off and having to deal with the huffing and puffing, yelling and slamming of things. It was better off for everyone if we just kept a low profile. Well, so we thought, since that was what we had been doing for years—tiptoeing around his mood changes.

I overheard Dillon speaking on the phone with Damien. The guest room was diagonal from my room and sound traveled easily throughout our house, having been built in the early 1900s. I quietly inched closer to my door in hopes of hearing more clearly what was being said: "If I leave, I can't come back. I'd have to take all my stuff. No, I don't think she'd tell, but I don't know."

Suddenly, the guest room door cracked opened, and Dillon made his way downstairs into the kitchen, just out of reach of my hearing any more of the phone conversation. I cracked my door open, and waited a few seconds to make it seem like the creaking sound was from Hershey opening the door like he always does by pressing against the doorknob with his nose. I slowly crawled to the top of the stairs to continue listening. I admit I shouldn't have been spying on him, but I was always a bit nosey and this time I felt justified, I wanted to know what was going on with my brother and what he was going to do next—or, maybe I just liked a little drama.

"We'd have to change the plates to do that though; we'd have to find some and switch them."

Change the plates on what? The car? What is he talking about?

Just then Mom came out of her room to use the bathroom and saw me lying at the end of the hall by the stairs.

"Riley, what are you doing?" she curiously asked.

I put my pointer finger up to my lips to signal her to be quiet, but it was too late. Dillon must have heard and abruptly told Damien he'd call him back later. He began walking down the hallway, out of the kitchen, towards the stairs and paused at the bottom patiently waiting to hear a sound. Thankfully, the stairwell was curved which obstructed his view of the top landing as I silently leaned against the corner of the wall. Dillon took a step up, again pausing. I held my breath praying for him to turn around, considering I had no explanation as to why I was lying there. I tried to think of reasons in my head, but it wasn't like I wore contacts or earrings that I could pretend to be searching for. Then again, those are the oldest tricks in the book and probably wouldn't have worked anyway.

As Dillon took another step up the stairs, Hershey came trotting down the hallway with his jingling tags hanging from his collar, walked right by me, and raced down the stairs to meet Dillon. With Hershey nudging his legs, Dillon took two steps down and headed back towards the kitchen, with Hershey following to be let outside. *Thank God,* I thought, finally exhaling in relief.

I felt as if I was in one of those Lifetime movies, where the suspicious girlfriend sneaks into her boyfriend's home while he's out to snoop through his things in order to find out if he's a murderer, only for him to return home unexpectantly. You know what happens next; the girl accidently drops something as she's trying to secretly exit, which captures the boyfriend's attention. The boyfriend slowly approaches the closed door behind which his girlfriend is nervously hiding; then just as he places his hand on the knob of the door, the doorbell or phone rings diverting his attention elsewhere, leaving the girlfriend time to escape. The only difference between those movies and this situation was that this was my reality—nothing was scripted.

My insomnia began that night. I twisted and turned in my bed for hours attempting to process and make sense of the conversation I had overheard. I couldn't understand what he was planning to do. *Changing plates . . . leaving and taking his things . . . not being able to come back. Why?*

Before I knew it, rays of light were slipping through the blinds and the sound of birds playfully chirping fluttered past my windows. It's amazing how the world can be so beautiful on the outside, while darkness, fear, and deception can linger on the other side of those blue-shuttered windows.

"Riley are you awake?" hesitantly asked Dillon as a soft knock echoed on my door.

I lay there as quiet as I could. I flung my covers over my head and turned to my side to look as if I were sleeping. I was nervous that he was going to confront me about listening in on the phone call or question me about the accusations Mom brought up to him the day before. He was my brother, and I didn't want to get in between anything or trigger one of his episodes by taking Mom's side.

Another hour or two had passed with me pretending to sleep in order to avoid interaction with Dillon, but my bladder could no longer cooperate. I crept up to my door to listen for any sounds or movements that would place Dillon nearby and was pleased to be met with silence. Quietly opening up my door, I took a step out and in that exact moment, the guest room door was pulled open almost as if our doors were in synch and connected to one another. Dillon's figure appeared.

"Hey! There you are! I was wondering if you could help me with something real quick," spoke Dillon.

"With what?" I answered sounding as normal as I possibly could.

"I need help moving my TV into the car."

TV? Why is he moving his TV into the car? What is he planning on doing? Where is he going? Is he leaving? Mom isn't going to like that—should I tell her? Was this what he meant on the phone last night when he said: "I don't think she would tell, but I don't know"?

"Yeah, let me just use the bathroom first and brush my teeth," I replied. I didn't know what to say in that moment. The look in his eyes was a look of over-excitement, a manic look I would even say. I needed time to stall. If I helped him bring the television down the stairs and load it into his car, Mom would be angry. But if I didn't, Dillon may throw a tantrum and I wasn't sure which one I was more afraid of. I took my time in the bathroom to think of what I was going to do when I heard heavy footsteps disappearing down the stairs and the front door closing.

I made my way back to my room and peaked out of the window which gave me a direct view of the cars parked in our driveway. Through the slits in the blinds, I saw Dillon load the 52-inch, flat-screen TV into the trunk of his car and watched his black Ford Escape pull out of the driveway for the last time, the sound of the gravel faintly shuffled under the tires.

"Where'd he go?" asked Mom from down the hall.

"I don't know . . . but he took the TV," I distantly answered.

CHAPTER 9:
VEGAS, HERE WE COME

The day finally came! August 6! Mom and I were on our way to Las Vegas for our little getaway. The vacation was originally supposed to consist of the three of us—Dillon, Mom, and me—but Dillon changed his mind at last minute and opted to stay home instead. Clearly with Damien. We didn't mind him not coming honestly; we both knew it would take a load off not having him with us. I mean, why would we want to tiptoe around someone who switched from fire to ice quicker than icy-hot? You know, it's that over-the-counter gel that some people use to relieve pain from minor injuries. The gel switches between cooling sensations to warming impressions, but anyways, yeah, back to what I was saying, basically we were just relieved that he wasn't going to be joining us.

Evidently our subtle excitement over Dillon's decision to not tag along completely backfired and kicked us in our asses, but I'll get more into that later on in the story, I promise.

Mom and I left for our Las Vegas adventure around 9:30 that Sunday morning, stopping for bagels before hitting the road. That was sort of a tradition ever since I was a kid, always stopping for bagels before going on vacations or even day trips to the beach or local amusement parks. This time, however, the bagels didn't fulfill the same type of enjoyment as it had done in the past. This time the bagels were flat and bland. It felt like a last-meal situation. I mean I don't really know how that feels. I'm sure it feels nothing like a stale bagel, but what I was getting at is that it felt like there was nothing to come back to after that. Like once it was done, it was done. Yet I swallowed the knot in my throat and carried on like my gut wasn't warning me that leaving would be a mistake.

Roughly an hour and a half into the drive Mom brought up the Dillon and Damien situation. She asked me my thoughts on what she should do when we return and how to go about everything. I wasn't sure why she was asking me; she was the adult, the parent, the person in charge but I guess she was lost and stuck between putting her foot down, risking the chance of losing her relationship with her son, or letting him slide consequence-free just like Mom and Dad have always done. Their constant avoidance for consequences for Dillon did nothing but continue to feed into his laziness, selfishness, and lack of motivation. I took my time answering the question and thought cautiously about which words to use. Mom was always sensitive when it came to Dillon. If I'd question why he wasn't working at twenty-eight years old, or how he was getting money or if I even brought up the possibility of Dillon being bipolar it would cause an instant fight. The last thing I needed was for an argument to break out before even reaching our destination, so I chose the safe route. I avoided her question directly and decided to vaguely voice my concerns instead.

"I don't want you to get mad when I say this, but it's been eating at me for a while now. I feel like something's going to happen, like Dillon is going to do something and I'm not sure what it is, but it's been sitting in my stomach for days now," I stuttered.

"What do you mean?" Mom curiously questioned.

"I don't know. I just think something is going to happen"

The conversation in the car became almost silent after that. I'm not sure if she had the same gut feeling, if she was thinking about what I said or if she was just not speaking to avoid an argument since I told her not to get mad at it.

But why would that even get her mad? I didn't say anything bad or degrading about Dillon. I was just concerned. He's my brother. And why doesn't she ever take my feelings seriously? I've expressed my growing fear of him to both Mom and Dad several times now over the last year or two and they just brush it off. Don't I matter? Don't my feelings or fear matter to them? Or is it all just about keeping Dillon in a calming mood?

We arrived at our hotel and casino around 2:45 in the afternoon. The sun was gleaming down, causing the pavement to glisten under its rays, almost as if glitter was sprinkled across it by a child. The dreadful feeling that I'd been carrying inside for days began to evaporate and exhilaration filled its place. We walked through the seven-foot-glass revolving doors into what seemed to be Disneyland for adults. The high dome-ceilings, pure white tiles leading up to the glossed-oak check-in counter with warm welcoming smiles stationed behind, eager to help us in any way possible and the sound of slot machine winnings drew my attention off of everything wrong in my life. In a way I guess one could say it gave me optimism for a new beginning. Looking back on it now, I can understand why people burn through their entire bank accounts in places like this and how it can become a type of addiction. The lingering possibility of one's whole life changing by a simple push of a button drives them to continue feeding their hard-earned money into the machines for the shot at leaving their problems behind once and for all.

Mom and I spent the rest of the night down at the machines and exploring the strip which the hotel was built on. There were carnival rides, concession stands, tourist shops, restaurants, and live music, all which seemed to fill the atmosphere with light. After winding down with a few Bahama Mamas and enjoying the cover bands that were playing, we decided to call it a night and head back up to our hotel room to get some well-needed rest.

The room was like a mini palace. A flat-screen TV that seemed to stretch from one end of the wall to the next was mounted in the center of the two queen-sized beds which were wholesome white and fluffed like a cloud. The mirror in the bathroom also doubled as a television. If you turned it on a portion of the glass would begin to darken and shows would begin to play while the other half of the glass remained reflective. Whoever thought of that idea had to be a genius, I loved being able to shower and take my time doing my hair and not having the burden of missing my shows.

That night was the best night's rest Mom or I had in a while. The mattresses were Tempur-Pedic, which shaped to and cradled our bodies. It felt nice being able to sleep not having to worry about Dillon and the tension that had been building. Actually, we slept so soundly that we didn't wake up until well into the afternoon hours the next day.

"Oh my God! How is it two o'clock already?" Mom said, with a playful laugh.

"Huh? Oh wow . . . is it really?" I questioned letting out a yawn and rubbing the crust from my eyes. I rolled back over, snuggling my face into the pillow in hopes to soak up a few extra minutes of that angelic sleep.

"Riley, start getting ready. We'll head down to the casino once I check in with your brother. I want to know how court went," Mom spoke.

"Mhm," I mumbled as I nudged my face deeper into the pillow and in that moment, I felt something soft hit the back of my head.

"Riley, c'mon—get up!"

"All right, all right, I'm up. I'm up," I reached my hand up, pulled off the pillow that was thrown at my head and jokingly tossed it back towards Mom before sluggishly untangling myself from the sheets and heading to the bathroom to change.

"Jesus! What is wrong with this damn kid?!" I heard Mom yell to herself.

"What? What happened?" I hollered from the bathroom.

"He didn't go to court. He said he didn't "feel" like it"

"What do you mean he didn't go?" I questioned as I walked back to the bed and sat down.

"Exactly what I said. Damien told him that there was no point in going, just to take the automatic guilty verdict by not showing up instead. Now he just has to pay the fines." Mom exhaled deeply.

"Yeah "he" has to pay the fines; he means you . . . but like who just doesn't show up for court?"

"Enough," Mom interrupted.

"I'm just saying; it's not like he has any money."

"I said enough," Mom repeated. I knew better than to keep pushing her after she repeated herself for a second time. Instead, I continued getting ready for our day. I didn't want to start an argument on our get away.

A week before we left, Dillon was pulled over for texting while driving and going sixty-one mph in a thirty-mph school zone. He came home with the tickets just like he did with all the other tickets he had accumulated over the past few years. He walked into Mom's room, told her he got a ticket, cried about how it wasn't his fault, and walked out with a smirk after Mom said she'd pay it. The red-light tickets were even worse. The county had installed cameras in almost all of the traffic lights around town which would snatch photos of any cars blowing through red lights. Well, Dillon clearly thought that he was above those considering that red-light tickets came in the mail almost weekly. The only problem with this was that the tickets came addressed to Mom, since the cars were under her name. If she didn't pay them, it would stack up against her, not Dillon. Yeah, sure, Mom would argue and scold Dillon constantly over it, yet that was always the extent of it. She'd yell, get frustrated, and a few hours later, it was like the ticket never happened. I mean, Dillon even got caught a few times hiding the tickets that came to the house for as long as he could until either I or Mom retrieved the mail only to see that the fines doubled or tripled due to late fees. Even then Dillon walked away consequence free, and "Mommy" paid for them.

That always irked me. Why didn't he ever have any consequences for his actions? It wasn't like the red-light tickets were an accident or a one-time thing. The link to the website to view the video footage of going through the intersections showed that his brake lights weren't even on; he didn't even attempt to stop. And that one time where he *was a good eighty to ninety feet back when the light changed to red, he almost caused an accident. The video showed a mini-van swerving into the next lane and slamming on their breaks to avoid Dillon as he drove through unamused. Like, who does that? Why didn't anyone care how reckless he was getting and how he had no appreciation for anything? And now he's just casually skipping out on court? Ha-ha, yeah, no wonder why; he's grown accustomed to having Mom and Dad bail him out every time he's in trouble—it doesn't matter what damage he does. Dillon is held accountable for nothing; nothing affects Dillon, Dillon doesn't do anything wrong. And he's smart too. He knows if he doesn't pay the $575 that a warrant will be put out for him and we all know Mom wouldn't let that happen to her "innocent," precious boy. If I ever pulled a stunt like that . . .*

"Riley, are you ready yet? I'm starving," Mom called out as she made her way to the door in the motorized wheelchair that she rented from the hotel.

"Yeah, one sec," I replied. I took a slow breath and put everything that just happened at the back of my mind.

CHAPTER 10:
SPAMMING TEXTS

Three hours went by and Mom was still stuck on the Dillon and court situation. I could see it in her face and tone that this was her breaking point; she was officially fed up with Dillon's behavior and Damien's influence. Maybe it was the fact that she was three drinks in, making her judgement cloudy, but she finally had the courage to confront Dillon on Damien's past and composed the text that she had been so hesitant to send.

Mom: How much do you know about Damien? - *Delivered at 6:26pm*
Dillon: Everything there is to know. - *Received at 6:27pm*
Mom: About his past? - *Delivered at 6:32pm*
Dillon: I know everything. If you looked him up, none of that was him
      - *Received at 6:33pm*
Mom: Huh? Who was it then? - *Delivered at 6:36pm*
Dillon: An old boyfriend manipulated him into it all. Damien is a really,
      really good guy. I love him so much Mommy and he's going to
      be around for a very long time - *Received at 6:38pm*
Dillon: He is my life - *Received at 6:38pm*
Dillon: He is my everything - *Received at 6:39pm*
Dillon: He is my reason - *Received at 6:39pm*
Dillion: So get used to it. - *Received at 6:39pm*

"Mom, you okay?" I asked, cutting her attention away from her phone. She had a distressed look, and her emotion began to hang on her face. I wasn't going to let Dillon ruin this too.

"Yeah, honey, I'm fine. Dillon's just in one of those moods," she responded, shaking her head and rolling her eyes.

In an attempt to get her mind off of Dillon and the stress, I suggested that we go walk down the strip to find somewhere to eat and expressed to her that it would be a smart idea to put her cellphone into her bag. I told her it was so she didn't lose it, but really, I just wanted her to stop falling into Dillon's games. Every few seconds her phone would *ding* and it was yet another text from Dillon. I tried to pay no mind to it and keep her interacted in the scenery and conversation. We were strolling down the Las Vegas strip; the site was absolutely beautiful, the tall buildings, flashing lights, the sound of water falling from the fountains and yet every few seconds was interrupted by the dinging of her phone. I offered to shut the sound off, but Mom was getting agitated and insisted on having her phone back.

Dillon: Why aren't you answering? - *Received at 7:10pm*
Dillon: I'm happy now. Does it hurt you to see me happy? - *Received at 7:10pm*
Dillon: He's all I need now and always - *Received at 7:11pm*
Dillon: Answer me. - *Received at 7:11pm*
Mom: I'm glad you are happy; that is all I could ever wish for you. Please stop; we are going to dinner now. Turning phone off - *Delivered 7:12pm*
Dillon: I will not stop - *Received at 7:13pm*
Dillon: You can't stop me - *Received at 7:13pm*
Dillon: I am grown now - *Received at 7:13pm*
Mom: Okay. I'm glad. - *Delivered at 7:14pm*

Mom softly shut her cell phone off and handed it to me to throw into her bag that was hanging on the back of her wheelchair. "Let's eat something good," she said as we continued down the strip. I could tell she didn't want to talk about what was going on with Dillon so I made no mention of it. I pointed out Joe's Seafood and before I could even ask if she was in the mood for fish she uttered, "Sounds good to me!"

I know one may be thinking why Mom didn't have much of a reaction to what Dillon was saying, why she gave short answers and didn't talk about it but that's because this wasn't new to her. We all had adapted to this type of behavior from Dillon. He would fixate on a certain topic and send text after text for hours on end going off about it and the more we didn't answer him the faster he would send them and the more hostile he would get. For example, about a year back, Mom was taking a nap while Dillon was cooking dinner. When dinner was ready, he decided to send Mom a text instead of calling out for her or going to her room to let her know. Mom's phone volume was silenced, meaning the text didn't wake her from her sleep and because she didn't answer him, he began sending text after text that—well . . . let me just show you.

Dillon: Dinner is ready - *Received at 5:41pm*

Dillon: I said dinner is ready. - *Received at 5:43pm*

Dillon: Either you eat with me or I kill myself - *Received at 5:44pm*

Dillon: Your choice - *Received at 5:44pm*

Dillon: Don't be selfish - *Received at 5:44pm*

Dillon: Be the kind of mother you were never able to be, Rita - *Received at 5:44pm*

Dillon: You didn't raise us on your own - *Received at 5:45pm*

Dillon: U were never there for us - *Received at 5:45pm*

Dillon: Emotionally - *Received at 5:45pm*

Dillon: Mentally - Received at 5:45pm

Dillon: u just got high and had cybersex with strangers all day - *Received at 5:45pm*

Dillon: while I did whatever the fuck I wanted to do - *Received at 5:46pm*

Dillon: Now you can't tell me what to do - *Received at 5:46pm*

Dillon: All you ever did was finger your pussy - *Received at 5:46pm*

Dillon: you're a perv - *Received at 5:47pm*

Dillon: who doesn't wash herself - *Received at 5:47pm*

Dillon: Mommy, it's time to eat - *Received at 5:47pm*

Mom was so well-adjusted to these kinds of bizarre and obsessive messages/statements from Dillon that when she did finally wake up to see them she just carried on with her day like none of it even happened. Same thing with Dad, too.

Dillon went on a spree one summer leaving dozens of messages on Dad's voicemail claiming that he was going to tell everyone that he touched him as a child (which is a complete lie by the way), making sexual comments/noises, threatening to kill him and in between all of his voicemails, Dillon would leave random ones saying that he loves him and hopes to see him soon. These messages went on for weeks during that summer. Dad finally blocked his number which just resulted in Dillon sending twenty to thirty text messages every few minutes from different texting app phone numbers that Dad just couldn't keep up with blocking them all. It was nearly impossible. Dillon wouldn't stop, even when Dad finally threatened to call the cops for harassment; it seemed like a game to him. Dillon leveled-up, leaving dozens of voicemails on the answering machine of Dad's house phone, many of which were actually encouraging Dad to call the police on him:

"Call the police, Daddy; come on, big boy, and I'll tell them how you touched me when I was younger"

Dillon most likely knew the threat from Dad was just a bluff. Dad never called the police. And just as quickly and randomly as these messages started, it ended just the same. They both acted as if it never occurred. It was normalized. It was just the way it was, according to Mom and Dad.

CHAPTER 11:
GONE, GONE, AND GONE

"No, Pete, no. I don't know—okay? He took his TV and he left." Mom's phone call with Dad whispered through the walls. "I just told you I don't know! Somewhere in Compton."

While Mom was on the phone figuring things out with Dad, I began cleaning up the mess that Dillon and Damien left behind in the kitchen. Honestly, with the number of boxes brought up from the basement, it was as if the kitchen was one of those back storage rooms in a warehouse. While picking up the containers, I noticed they were oddly light, and many were torn open. It only took a few moments to realize what exactly was going on: they weren't cleaning like he says; they were helping themselves and shuffling through the house, taking more than just Mom's money. I ran up the stairs with one of the boxes and cautiously knocked on Mom's door. "Yeah, come in," Mom called out. I opened the door and stood in the doorway, immediately Mom knew from my expression that something was wrong. "Pete, I'll call you back. I'll call you back," Mom rushed the words out of her mouth and hung up the phone.

"What is it now?" Mom questioned as she struggled to sit herself up in bed.

"I'm not really sure what it is, but those boxes they brought up from the basement are all half-emptied and this one just has a few broken pieces of glass in it. It looks like they were plates or something."

"Plates? They're not white with gold and blue trimmings, are they?" Mom asked. It was clear she wanted the answer to be no. I took a deep breath in, reached my hand into the box and pulled out a shattered piece and held it up for her to see. Her eyes closed; shoulders dropped, slowly putting her hand up, signaling me to stop. I put the box down onto the floor and sat on the end of her bed, placing my hand onto her leg for whatever support I could give her. Turns out those dishes were a wedding gift from her parents, pure China and gold. The unfortunate reality finally sunk in. Dillon and Damien ransacked the house and selfishly grabbed whatever they could, anything of value. I knew the remaining boxes in the kitchen would prove the same thing. There was nothing more that I could do but continue through the mess and uncover what else was missing so that we could glue together the full picture.

Vintage cameras from the 1950s, ones that had the backdrop and all the finishings that were from my great uncle, gone. Boxes of German World War Two war bonds from my great grandparents, gone. An original Tiffany lamp passed down from her grandmother, gone. China dishes, gone. Dozens of binders stacked with old baseball and football cards that Mom had been collecting since she was a kid, gone. An entire John F. Kennedy collection, gone. A lock box containing some of my grandmother's jewelry, gone. A Beatles collection, gone. My chrome cast, gone. An old laptop of mine, gone. The only thing left were crumbs of little reminders of the damage that was done.

But why would he do this? What would possess Dillon to clear out the house as if it were a liquidation sale? Wasn't the five thousand dollars enough? What did he need the money for? It's obvious he wanted to make a profit since he only took things that held a price tag. But why? And why target Mom? She's done nothing but go above and beyond for us; she always gave us money when we needed it. She always got us whatever we wanted, like wasting three grand once on a leather jacket that he desired. She was hesitant at first, but he begged, and he got it. What was the need to steal? The only thing she had to live off of was the money that was left to her and now even that was gone. Was this a game to him? Was this his end goal all along? How long had he been plotting this? This visibly wasn't a "in-the- heat-of-a-moment" event; this was undoubtingly planned and drawn out. But why? Why? Why—and the

NERVE of him to come back into this house like NOTHING happened? It's clear now that this was the reason his response to Mom telling him that things were missing was "like what?" He was that confident of himself that he could pull this over on us that he bounced back into the house making Mom tea like we were a picture-perfect family, only to take off the next day with the TV. I guess it couldn't fit into the car the first time. He must truly believe that he's untouchable. That he's made of gold. That he's above all.

"Find out where the hell he is! Do you hear me? Do you hear me, Pete?!" Mom screamed through the phone.

"Everything is gone, Pete! Everything!" she continued.

I wasn't sure what to make of this or how to help. I sat downheartedly against the wall of my bedroom, the one which separated my room from hers so that I could hear the conversation with Dad clearly. Not like it was hard to hear, I'm sure her screaming could be heard from outside. The wall vibrated against my back from the force of anger bursting from her voice when she spoke. I wanted to send Dillon a message. I wanted to say something to him. I wanted to tell him off. I was furious. I was betrayed. I wondered what else was missing that we just hadn't realized yet. I never in a million years thought my brother would steal from me.

I remember when we were kids, we lived around the corner from a gas station and Mom gave us money to get slushies or candy. Dillon and I walked, I held his hand when we crossed the streets, and we talked about what we were going to do that day. When we finally arrived at the gas station, we got our slushies and noticed little rubber balls in a display box on the counter. The balls were the size of tennis balls attached to a black stretchy string with a wrist band on the end. I guess it was similar to the idea of yoyos, each ball had a different design; some were baseballs, soccer balls, basketballs, etc. Both of us picked one up, I picked up the baseball and Dillon chose the soccer ball. However, at the register we were short two dollars. Dillon looked down at me and with no hesitation put his back. On our walk back home, Dillon opened up the package and attached the wrist band to my wrist so I could play with it. He never once asked for a turn and when I would leave it lying around the house he never once touched it. He never once took the last ice pop from me, or the last juice box. He would even give me back the loose change left in my pockets when he would do laundry. He never once took from me growing up; why would he start now? It's not like I didn't share with him. When Dillon didn't have money to buy Dad and our stepmom Christmas presents, he asked if I could add his name to the ones I had bought, which I did with no reluctance. When he asked to use my chrome cast, I always let him. Sure, he could have taken more from me, like my jewelry or my money, and I realize my missing chrome cast, an old laptop from high school, and the USB wires to my speakers are relatively small compared to all that he took from Mom, but my anger was more about the sense of security taken from me than the actual things themselves. I was crushed just by the simple fact that he would take from me at all.

"Yeah, Pete, and you know what? You can tell him that I'm reporting that fucking car stolen because that kid doesn't fucking answer me. That's bullshit! If he stole from you, things would be different." I wish I could hear what was being said on the other end; it sounded like he was trying to lessen the situation and mediate like he always does. Dad always tries to be the middleman and satisfy both sides, but I couldn't imagine his reasoning for this. How could he possibly be trying to convince her that Dillon stealing five thousand dollars in cash and thousands more in valuables is anything less severe than it actually is? This wasn't like the time Dillon got suspended from school for smoking in the girl's bathroom with his friends, or the time he got caught shoplifting a shirt from the mall, where Dad downplayed both instances and talked Mom down. He convinced her that it was just a thing teenagers do and that it could have been worse. Just like that, Dillon was off the hook. Oh, and the time during Dillon's freshman year of high school when he went to a party and Dad received a call from his friends panicking, telling him that he needed to come pick Dillon up; he nearly had alcohol poisoning. Dad had to carry him over his shoulder out of the house while Dillon puked down his back, yet the next morning none of it was ever discussed because Dad again claimed it could have been worse.

No matter what either me or Dillon did, it never fazed Dad. He'd show slight frustration or anger in the moment but would quickly relax and say, "It could have been worse." It's like ever since losing Shane, nothing we did could top that. We were still alive and in his eyes, that's all that mattered.

I get that. I really do. I get that things could always be worse than what they actually are, like losing your child, but at some point, somewhere along the way, don't we need to be held accountable for our actions? How can he let this one slide? Doesn't he realize that there's a deeper issue here? Yes, the situation could be worse. Yes, Dillon could be dead right now, but you know what? He's not dead. He's here and alive and he robbed his mother. Its time he stops downplaying and disregarding everything that his son does. There's no excuse for this. There really isn't.

"Riley, come in here, please," Mom called out. I took a second to get up so she wouldn't hear that I was against the wall trying to listen and headed to her room. She asked me to go into the filing cabinet in her closet and look for the folder with our car information in it. I opened the top draw to her dresser to grab the key for the filing cabinet, only to find that it wasn't there. I rushed the drawer closed and headed towards the closet. "What's wrong?" Mom questioned. I continued towards her closet without answering, I didn't want to make any accusations until I knew for sure if Dillon had something to do with it. I yanked open the door and there it was. The filing cabinet pulled open with the key dangling from the lock. Papers and folders spread across the floor. Mom kept the most important of important papers in that cabinet. There, she had all our birth certificates, death certificates, banking information, life insurance forms, house insurance, papers for our cars, medical documents, our passports . . .

"Son of a bitch," my voice cracked.

"Riley, what? What happened?"

I continued to ignore Mom and shuffle through the top drawer of the filing cabinet where our passports were kept. I pulled mine and Mom's, but Dillon's was gone.

"Well, he took his passport." I mimicked a surprised tone.

"Are you kidding me? Is anything else touched?" she asked as she reached for her walker to make her way over to the closet to see for herself. She struggled to make her way over and upon reaching the doorway, she closed her eyes, took a deep breath, and exhaled while shaking her head.

"Oh my God, Riley . . . you're going to have to bring those papers over to me. I need to sort through them to see what's missing; I don't even know where to start."

I scooped up the folders and loose papers and placed them onto her bed. I just stood there not knowing what to say, muttering out if she needed any help. Mom quickly turned her head away from me as her lips began to quiver, shaking her head "No."

"Do you need anything?" I asked.

"Just—just leave me alone," she snapped back.

I was timid, but I turned and left the room, softly closing her bedroom door behind me. I could hear her begin to cry which caused my heart to sink into my gut. About an hour later, I overheard her make phone call after phone call asking to cancel out credit cards and inquiring about recent transactions. A few phone calls later, her voice began to crack and her attempts to hold her composure failed. She abruptly ended the call and the tears started to flow. I've never had the heart to ask her if he took any of her credit cards or if there was any banking information missing. I figured enough damage was done and I didn't need to add to it.

It was no surprise that Mom skipped dinner that night; she hadn't had much of an appetite the last two days. Although she refused the offer, I made her a cup of hot tea and two slices of toast with butter on it and placed it on her nightstand anyway. I thought maybe it would help ease her stomach. She was lying on her side, facing the wall with the papers stacked on her bed. I gave her a kiss on the cheek and told her I loved her. Upon leaving her room, my phone vibrated in my back pocket. It was from Dad.

Dad: Did your mother really report Dillon's car stolen? Honey, I really
     need to know -*Received at 8:42pm*
Me: She hasn't said anything to me. But if she told you she did, she
     probably did - *Delivered at 8:44pm*
Dad: Honey . . . if she did, he can get arrested. Is that what she wants?
     - *Received at 8:45pm*

I didn't even bother responding back. I didn't want to get into the middle of it and I can't believe that he was trying to make it seem like Mom was the one at fault if she actually reported the car stolen. Like what? Of course, she doesn't want Dillon to be arrested; what parent wants that for their child? But considering the circumstances, I would have done the same thing—look at everything he took from her. And besides, the car is registered in her name, the insurance is in her name, she's the one who pays for it. If anything were to happen to the car, it would ultimately fall onto her and quite frankly who knows what Dillon may do. It comes to the point where she has to protect herself too.

CHAPTER 12:
HIDDEN BEHIND A KEYBOARD: PART 1

The sun creaked through the blinds of my bedroom window, reflecting a shimmering light gleaming off of the walls and onto my face. Pulling my blanket over my head to block out the light, I wasn't ready to see what hell this day would bring. It was only day four since returning from our Vegas getaway, yet it felt like years had passed. I had no motivation left or any will to get up. It seemed Dillon took that too. I must have dozed off for another hour or two before I was awakened by soft nudges on my cheek. "Hershey, five more minutes," I mumbled as I extended my arm out over the edge of the bed to pet his head, only he leaped up and plummeted onto my stomach. My eyes shot open, coughing to catch my breath. "All right, all right Hershey," I coughed. He jumped down, wagging his tail excitedly waiting to be let outside. He raced down the spiral staircase as I slugged behind. It was a quiet morning, and I didn't want to wake Mom if she were still sleeping; she very much needed the rest, and I needed the break.

I stepped out of the sliding glass doors and onto the back patio with my throw blanket wrapped around my shoulders to get some fresh air while waiting for Hershey. It was a beautiful Saturday morning with a bright-blue sky and a warm breeze. A plane flew by, disappearing into a cloud as jealousy soaked in. I wished I were on that plane, going anywhere but here. I wished I could just up and leave, not having to worry about what was going on and just leave it all behind. I wished life was as simple as that: to disappear into a cloud. I tried to be just as quiet coming into the house as I was going out to avoid Mom hearing that I was up. I didn't feel like socializing yet and wanted some more time to myself to unwind but our stairs tended to creek and upon reaching my door, Mom yelled out for me to come into her room.

I hung my head in loss and made my way down the hall. Mom asked if I could look up the number for our cell phone company so that she could cancel Dillon's service from her line. This wasn't new territory; she had shut my service off a handful of times growing up when I would misbehave but she had never done it to Dillon. Dillon always got off the hook with things by both parents, yet they would come down on me twice as hard when I got into trouble. It was like they were punishing me for Dillon's mistakes as well since they were always reluctant to confront his actions. Before I could even get the chance to ask her why she was shutting off his phone service, Mom handed me her phone to read the texts that Dillon was sending.

Dillon: You stupid fucking bitch - *Received at 8:51am*

Dillon: I'll go out right now and sell the car - *Received at 8:58am*

Dillon: I know people - *Received at 9:00am*

Dillon: Taking away your son's only means of transportation; do you feel big now? -*Received at 9:00am*

Mom: I'm sorry you feel that way. - *Delivered at 9:03am*

Dillon: Selfish piece of shit. Takes from whoever she can - *Received at 9:04am*

Dillon: You will not take from me anymore - *Received at 9:04am*

Mom: Good. And I will not give to you anymore. Shutting off your phone service as we speak - *Delivered at 9:06am*

Mom: And I am telling you one last time that every single thing that you took from this house better be returned here or I'll be making police reports for that as well. - *Delivered at 9:07am*

I handed the phone back to Mom, not wanting to read whatever else he was spitting at her and read off the phone number to the phone company. I wandered over to her window while I waited for the phone call to end, looking up at the sun trying to grab a glimpse of hope from its rays. A cloud soon found its way in front, dimming the ground below and casting me in its shadow. I turned to look at

Mom and then back towards the window. Right then and there I knew the storm had yet to come. Mom finally finished the call and put her hands out for a hug. I quickly made my way back over to the bed and wrapped my arms around her. "I love you," she said. I squeezed her tighter before letting go and sitting down next to her.

"So . . . did you really report the car stolen?" I cautiously asked. I wasn't sure if she actually did, considering this wasn't the only time she has made that threat. Her favorite thing to take away from me when I got into trouble or acted up once I reached that age was my car. She would threaten to cancel the insurance so that I couldn't drive and if I called her bluff and took the car anyway, she would claim she was going to report it stolen. All of which she never did, which is safe to say why Dillon wasn't taking her warning seriously. He must have assumed that because Mom never followed through on those threats with me when I would take the car against her word that she wouldn't follow through on it with him. But then again, I never stole thousands of dollars from her, robbed her house clean, or threatened to kill her.

"No Riley, I didn't. I don't know what the hell to do about anything and your father keeps begging me not to."

Not even five minutes went by before Mom's phone began to ding in clusters, lighting up the screen with messages.

Dillon: This is an emergency - *Received at 11:12am*
Dillon: Turn my phone back on - *Received at 11:12am*
Dillon: RIGHT NOW - Received at 11:12am
Dillon: Right now, bitch, don't make me mad - *Received 11:13am*

Mom's face drained pale while staring down at her phone in hand. "How—how is he still texting me?" she hopelessly asked. She didn't understand that with smartphones one could send text messages as long as they were connected to Wi-Fi, and that it didn't require activation through a phone company. I explained to her that he wouldn't be able to send messages or receive messages in areas that Wi-Fi was unavailable or even make phone calls. It wasn't like when we were kids and shutting off the service to our phones meant we could get no use from them; technology has greatly improved since then.

Dillon: If I die, this will be your fault - *Received at 11:18am*
Dillon: My phone is my only life line - *Received at 11:18am*
Dillon: My death on your hands - *Received at 11:19am*
Dillon: Mommy, this is life or death. I am not playing - *Received at 11:20am*
Dillon: Turn my phone back on right fucking now - *Received at 11:20am*
Dillon: You selfish cunt - *Received at 11:21am*
Dillon: Please turn my phone back on if u want any chance of me surviving - *Received at 11:26am*
Dillon: This is not a joke - *Received at 11:26am*
Dillon: I'm not playing - *Received at 11:26am*

I advised Mom not to respond to anything that he was saying, to just block him out and pay no mind to it. It was obvious he wasn't going to stop but maybe telling her to ignore him was the wrong advice. We all knew ignoring him just added more fuel to the fire, but so did responding. He longed for attention and wasn't going to stop until he got it. The messages quickly became cringeworthy and sickening to read, one after the other with no time to blink in between. The massive number of texts spamming through caused Mom's phone to freeze. It took a good twenty minutes to finally get it to restart and turn back on again; nonetheless, the texts continued.

Dillon: Your life is over bitch - *Received at 12:01pm*
Dillon: You're fucking dead - *Received at 12:01pm*
Dillon: You better watch your back - *Received at 12:01pm*
Dillon: Your crippled back - *Received at 12:01pm*
Dillon: You better lock up the house REAL GOOD - *Received at 12:02pm*

Dillon: You won't live through this week I PROMISE you - *Received at 12:02pm*

Dillon: I want NOTHING more than to stab you repeatedly - *Received at 12:02pm*

Dillon: Fucking watch you bleed - *Received at 12:02pm*

Dillon: Fucking laugh at your pain - *Received at 12:02pm*

Dillon: Fucking see you covered in blood - *Received at 12:03pm*

Dillon: Fucking choke you with my dick - *Received at 12:03pm*

Dillon: Fucking rape you - *Received at 12:03pm*

Dillon: Give you AIDS - *Received at 12:03pm*

Dillon: Fucking suffocate you - *Received at 12:03pm*

Dillon: Fucking kill you - *Received at 12:04pm*

Dillon: Fucking burn you - *Received at 12:04pm*

Dillon: Watch your bones fall to ashes - *Received at 12:04pm*

Dillon: Light your home on fire - *Received at 12:04pm*

Dillon: I'm going to kill you - *Received at 12:04pm*

Dillon: Murder you - Received at 12:05pm

Dillon: Fucking slit your throat - *Received at 12:05pm*

Dillon: Fucking pillage you - *Received at 12:05pm*

Dillon: I will fucking slit your throat open like a goat - *Received at 12:06pm*

Dillon: Mommy my goat - Received at 12:06pm

Dillon: Can't wait to see you on your death bed - *Received at 12:06pm*

Dillon: Hope you bleed to death - *Received at 12:06pm*

Dillon: Feed you blueberries and watch your fucking throat close - *Received at 12:06pm*

Dillon: Struggle for air - *Received at 12:07pm*

Dillon: I hate you - Received at 12:07pm

Dillon: I hate you so fucking much - *Received at 12:07pm*

Dillon: You did this to me - *Received at 12:07pm*

Dillon: You raised me like this then turned your back on me - *Received at 12:08pm*

Dillon: You fucking cunt - *Received at 12:08pm*

Dillon: You're crippled because you deserve it - *Received at 12:08pm*

Dillon: It matches what is in your heart - *Received at 12:08pm*

Dillon: ANSWER ME - Received at 12:08pm

Dillon: Your love is crippled and conditional - *Received at 12:08pm*

Dillon: You deserve whatever life sends your way - *Received at 12:09pm*

Dillon: Mommy please die - *Received at 12:10pm*

Dillon: Do us all a favor - *Received at 12:10pm*

Dillon: I'm going to steal everything I can from you - *Received at 12:10pm*

Dillon: Mommy. Please turn my phone back on - *Received at 12:11pm*

Dillon: Don't make me hurt you - *Received at 12:11pm*

All right, yeah. . . . let's stop the texts there; I'm sure you get the point. I can't even begin to describe the look of brokenness that overcame Mom. There had to be hundreds of texts coming through; we couldn't keep up with them. Reading the messages instantly made her sick and I could hear Mom vomiting in the bathroom. I went to knock on the bathroom door to see if she was okay when my phone started blowing up with texts. My immediate thought was Dillon but was relieved to see it was only Liana. She asked what was going on and if I was okay, I asked her what she was talking about since I didn't get the chance yet to tell anyone about the vulgar messages Dillon was sending to Mom. Liana told me to check his updated status on his SocialFriends' page profile right away; she claimed he was making threats and accusing Mom of being a drug addict.

Standing outside of the bathroom door I directly pulled up the SocialFriends app on my phone, SocialFriends was a social media platform where friends and family could follow each other and stay connected through status updates, photos, and messages. I was anxious to get on to see what Liana was speaking of; Dillon had all of our family and friends on his page, and I could only imagine what they would be thinking. The app finally loaded. I clicked Dillon's name and stared in disbelief. He had about four or five statuses dedicated to the situation. I continued to scroll through his page, he posted nonsense such as claiming Mom had always been jealous of him since the day that he was born because the attention was no longer on her, but him. Another post stating that he is finally free from years of "abuse" and can no longer be controlled. One post in particular, however, topped them all:

Dillon Venturi: Rita Venturi is nothing but a disgraceful pill addict. Pain killers especially. She has been a user my entire life, altering her abilities to be a mother—ignoring my basic needs and helplessness. I was forced to raise myself in a home with nowhere to turn, no mother to comfort her baby boy. I am only as good to her as with what I have to offer. The second I have nothing to offer I am once again worthless and useless to her. Now that she can no longer get her fix, she is creating lies and kicked me to the curb. She has wished death on me, emotionally and physically abused me and forced me to sell and buy drugs. I am now a man, a strong (and dangerous) one; I will NOT tolerate this kind of disgustful behavior from the one person who was supposed to protect and love me. Yet my kind and loving heart once again became my downfall when I had the chance to drain her bank accounts dry. I should have done it when the opportunity rose. It's rightfully mine and it is what she deserves. The only message I have for her would be just watch what you say about me . . . because I have ears all over, and I know all of your dirtiest secrets. And the illegal ones. I have the house watched, like vultures waiting for their prey. Waiting on my command, your fate is in my hands. Oh, I'm going to be just fine without you, sweetheart. Will you be fine without me? Xoxo, Mommy's little boy. - *Posted 45 minutes ago*

It wasn't the post itself that got me; it was the comments that people were leaving encouraging him to continue with this behavior that was sickening. There were forty-six comments at that moment, but more were being added by the second making it difficult to read due to new remarks pushing up the screen. I scrolled through, skimming the comments to get the gist of what was going on and being said.

Samantha Link: What a bitch she is. Always has been, so sorry you
have to go through that. Text me - *Posted 30 minutes ago*
Archer LaCoco: Can't believe your mother is addicted to
painkillers . . . the opioid epidemic is a huge problem around
the US! All the OxyContin, heroin, etc. - *Posted 26 minutes ago*
Dillon Venturi: It's heartbreaking. I tried for years to help her. But one
can only do so much and unless she wants to help herself,
there's nothing I can do. When I had a conversation with her
about going to rehab she went batshit crazy, accusing me and
my boyfriend of stealing from her. Now I WISH I had milked
her dry and emptied out her bank accounts. My name used to
be linked on all her accounts and I could be living like a king
right now! Never again will my heart get in the way of myself.
- *Posted 25 minutes ago*
Samuel O'Conner: Dillon, what is going on over there? Can't we all
just get along? - *Posted 23 minutes ago*
Archer LaCoco: Sounds like your mother has literally dug her own
grave, twelve feet under. I always believe fire should be met
with fire. Justice needs to be done! - *Posted 23 minutes ago*
Dillon Venturi: She will burn to crumbs! - *Posted 22 minutes ago*

"Riley! Please come here!" Mom called out as she was
finally making her way out from the bathroom and into her
bedroom. I quickly put my phone into my pocket and
hurried into her room to see what she wanted. "What is he
posting?" she anxiously asked and explained that her
friends and family kept texting her to see if she was okay
and what was happening between her and Dillon. Friends
reaching out and sending her information on drug rehabs
and counseling which she blatantly did not have use for
since this whole "drug addiction" was a made-up scenario
created by Dillon's attention-seeking needs. Sorrow took
over my face as I sat down next to her, pulling up his
SocialFriends page to read through his posts and the
comments with her.

Archer LaCoco: It's appalling how family can backstab you. I don't
tolerate that whatsoever and I stand by and support anyone

who's a victim of that. Whatever the consequences must be -
Posted 35 minutes ago
Samantha Link: She's had it coming! - *Posted 35 minutes ago*
Dillon Venturi: Thanks, guys. It has taken a lot out of me to stand up
to my abuser. Now the truth is out there and will set me free -
Posted 34 minutes ago

I glanced over at Mom and saw that she was crumbling. I've never seen someone look so lost and shattered before. I couldn't let this go on, I had to say something. How was I supposed to just sit back and read through Dillon dragging Mom through the mud on social media? I had to finally confront Dillon; I couldn't stay out of it any longer. I refused to let Mom sit and listen to the appalling lies and accusations against her with no one coming to her defense. The days of tiptoeing over Dillon and his moods have come to an end. Enough is enough. I stopped reading and began to type out a message. Mom told me to let the situation be since I knew that any kind of response would only engulf his flame, but anger consumed my judgement and, nonetheless, I continued on with my post:

Riley Venturi: Nice, Dillon. Should I post the death threats you've
been sending her all because she shut your phone service off?
You stole so much from her that I don't even know where to
begin. Money? Like really? You steal from your mother who
has done EVERYTHING for you then come on here and make
outrageous claims and talk about "burning her to crumbs"?
And for every one of you supporting his behavior, you are just
as sick and disgusting as he is. - *Posted 30 seconds ago*

Looking back on the situation now I probably should have listened to Mom when she told me to stay out of it because it only took a few minutes for hell to break out.

Dillon Venturi: Stay out of this, Riley. There is no reason to have beef
between us. I would of course share my inheritance with you.
No need to worry, little one. - *Posted 1 minute ago*

Dillon Venturi: Better yet, do it! I changed my mind, post my texts to her! Let's play that game! I'll win - *Posted 30 seconds ago*

Archer LaCoco: Give her those death threats, baby! May karma burn her like never before! - *Posted 30 seconds ago*

Archer LaCoco: He has every right to feel that way, Riley. There is no greater sin than BETRAYAL. There is the nineth circle of hell for people guilty of that, and Rita Venturi is heading straight for it. I am very tempted to take matters into my own hands. - *Posted just now*

Riley Venturi: And who the hell are you? He has every right to feel whatever he feels but that DOESN'T mean it's okay to threaten to kill people, rape them, and slice them open. Everything he's claiming is a lie anyway. My mother doesn't do drugs, but the hundreds of drug baggies and syringes found in his room clearly show that he does. My Mom isn't the one with crack pipes in her drawers. - *Posted just now*

Dillon Venturi: Thanks, Archer. My family doesn't know how to contribute anything but hysterics and melodramatic acts to any situation. They just use and abuse until you're covered in bruises (emotional and physical). - *Posted just now*

Dillon Venturi: And just to clarify, the "hundreds" of baggies are a collection from the past three years. Also, they are meth pipes. Crack is whack! - *Posted just now*

Is this a joke? He's making a joke out of this? I don't find anything funny about finding drugs and seeing him threaten Mom text after text. How are people sticking up for him? Who the hell is this Archer guy? I don't even know what to do anymore. This is breaking Mom apart; what do I do? What am I supposed to do? How do I make him stop? How do I make any of this stop? He needs help. He needs so much fucking help, and no one is doing anything! People are cheering him on like it's a damn circus! What's it going to take? For Dillon to actually kill Mom? Will that do it? Will that make people stop and realize how serious this actually is? I've seen this anger, this rage building for years and no one listened. And now? Now he burst; he exploded like a bomb sending currents in all directions and there's no telling which one will get the hit. It's coming, yet no one is running.

Riley Venturi: Wow . . . it's sad that you find humor in YOUR drug addiction. Either this is all a joke to you, Dillon, or you honestly believe these little lies in your head to be true. And if that is the case, my heart breaks for you. It really does. - *Posted 30 seconds ago*

Dillon Venturi: The only thing I believe to be true is the truth and Rita Venturi WILL be held responsible for her actions. I will slice and dice her to pieces until she repents for her sins - *Posted just now*

Archer LaCoco: Slice and dice, baby! - *Posted just now*

Archer LaCoco: Chop 'em up, bitch! Riley, you'll be getting it, too! - *Posted just now*

Archer LaCoco: Chop 'em up and watch them burn! - *Posted Just now*

CHAPTER 13:
ARCHER LACOCO

Mom began to ask me who Archer was, but my guess was just as good as hers. I had never heard of him before, and Dillon had never mentioned him. Archer seemed to have the same type of mental issues as Dillon, considering the things that he was saying and encouraging Dillon to follow through with his threats. I decided to search his name to see if I could find any information on who he was and if he was truly a menace. Instantaneously, web pages began popping up regarding psychics and astrologists—something that Dillon was passionate about. Dillon had a tendency to obsess over psychic readings, astrology, and the spiritual world, but deeper than the average person. He would actually live his daily life based on what his readings were from whatever psychic he contacted the night before or prediction he read online to the point where it became more of a dependence than anything.

Now that I think of it, he would spend hours a day chatting with online psychic services which those services commonly charge by the minute. We all know by now that Dillon didn't have a job, so I'd say it's a safe bet to assume he was using Mom's credit cards without her realizing, although she did catch a charge for three hundred and something dollars one time linked to one of those sites. Dillon, of course, pled that it wasn't him and that someone must have hacked into her account. As pathetic as it sounds, Mom believed him and disputed the charge with the bank.

Would he be that stupid though to continue to put charges onto her card hoping she wouldn't realize anymore? Or was he doing smaller charges at a time so she wouldn't pick up on it? If not, how was he getting the money for it? He had to be doing something. Was this why I found a bunch of bank statements addressed to Mom hoarded in his room? Was he intercepting the mail to prevent her from seeing what was being done? I mean she wasn't too tech savvy so there is the possibility that he knew she wouldn't bother checking her bank statements online, but would he have chanced that? Did he actually take the time to plan that out? I wish I paid more attention to the charges listed on the statements when I found them instead of aimlessly tossing them in the trash when I realized how old they were. Or what about that debit card I found in his room? Dillon didn't have a job; Dillon didn't have any funds. As far as Mom and I knew, he didn't have a bank account. All the times he would get checks from our grandparents on birthdays and holidays he would have Mom cash them for him because he couldn't without an account. So how did he have his own debit card? Wait . . . what if he opened an account to store the money that he was quietly snatching from Mom all these years and used that account to fund these chats? Was he really that invested and motivated in this? Did he actually take the time to plan this entire thing out? How long was this going on for? What else did he do? What . . .

"Riley, did you find anything on Archer yet?" Mom called out from her room.

I directed my attention back to my computer screen to finish the search on Archer. Interestingly enough, I came across a link to public court documents regarding threats and assault on an individual two years prior. While reading further, the individual appeared to have been a client of his who began questioning his practices and doubting the information that Archer was preaching to him. Archer apparently didn't take too kindly to this person calling him a fake and began to send him messages about how he was going to harm and kill him. The individual stopped responding and associating with Archer until Archer showed up uninvited to his home and pulled out a knife. I continued my search to see if I could find any more similar cases but all I came across were several comments and posts on his social media pages from previous clients claiming him as a fraud and that he threatened to put curses on them when they began questioning his creditability. A few posts even accused Archer of diving into black magic, which I honestly suspected Dillon of as well.

Dillon became increasingly interested in the afterlife and spiritual realms. About a year ago, we found him in the kitchen one night finishing up a homemade Ouija board that he crafted out of wood. Mom immediately demanded he get rid of it but to this day, I'm not sure if we'll ever know what actually happened to it. I wouldn't be surprised if it were still stored and hidden somewhere in the house. I'd often times even overhear Dillon repeating strange chants in his bedroom during odd hours of the night while burning sage. He claimed to be cleansing the air; however, it seemed to be a nightly occurrence and he would only do this to his room, not the rest of the house. It was as if he was dipping his toes into this dark afterworld and after he was done playing, he would sage his area to prevent anything from lingering around. One night, I stumbled upon him climbing into a wooden chest in the basement which Mom and Dad had always warned us not to touch growing up because the previous owner had supposedly told them when they bought the house that there was paranormal activity connected to it.

Mom and Dad claimed that the owner disclosed to them before they went through with closing on the house that the chest was left there when he had purchased the home twenty years before and that he had actually sold that chest to four different people during a yard sale but each of them coincidently forgot it or left without it. He also said that one person did end up taking it with them but later that day it reappeared on the lawn, so he placed it back into its spot in the back corner of the basement and left it alone, which we all did as well. Well . . . until Dillon decided to mess with it, of course. I was walking down the stairs to the basement to do a load of laundry when I turned the corner and spotted Dillon at the other end standing in front the chest. I kept quiet to make my presence unknown so that I could see what he was doing with it. I mean, we were always told to just leave it undisturbed and not to pay any mind to it, so I wanted to see why he was staring down at it with a glow in his eye. Next thing I know Dillon creaked open the lid and inhaled deeply while flowing his arms in an upward motion over the chest as if he was scooping the air from the trunk into his lungs before stepping into it, lying down, closing the lid and began humming. I slowly made my way back up the stairs and never mentioned what I saw to Dillon or even my parents simply because I couldn't make sense of any of it and in all honesty, I felt very disturbed and uneasy for a while after experiencing that scene.

Mom yet again yelled out to me asking if I found anything on Archer. I grabbed my laptop and hustled back into her bedroom so that I could read to her the articles that I had found. We agreed that Archer sounded psychotic and although she became worried with the threats that were being made, she found some relief in the fact that he lived across the country all the way in Vermont. Vermont was a good twenty-four-hour-plus car ride from us with no stops or traffic along the way; the only aspect of it that worried us in that moment was his influence on Dillon. There was no telling what Dillon was going to do and we feared that with Archer's influence and encouragement that Dillon might follow through.

CHAPTER 14:
HIDDEN BEHIND A KEYBOARD: PART 2

My phone continued to ping with notifications from replies on Dillon's post on SocialFriends. There had to be about thirty new comments from when I had last replied. I scrolled through and skimmed quickly to catch myself up on what was happening when I noticed comments from my Aunt Denise questioning Archer's definition on justice.

Archer LaCoco: Dillon, I will stand by your side with whatever means you must take to deliver justice and to reclaim your peace. - *Posted 5 minutes ago*

Archer LaCoco: I personally would go with a mixture of stabbing and burning to give that bitch a sense of the pain that she put you through. - *Posted 5 minutes ago*

Dillon Venturi: Burn holes in her skin with the ends to her cigarettes - *Posted 4 minutes ago*

Denise Lamberti: Archer, cheering on someone who is threatening to kill someone else is NEVER a good thing. - *Posted 3 minutes ago*

Archer LaCoco: It is and always will be justified. You and Riley standing for the abuser is just as sinful as Rita herself. - *Posted 2 minutes ago*

Denise Lamberti: Justifiable? Wow . . . never knew threatening murder in this case was justified but that just shows what kind of person you are - *Posted 1 minute ago*

Archer LaCoco: *chop chop chop* here comes the Los Angeles Horror! - *Posted 1 minute ago*

Archer LaCoco: For best results may I suggest the dismemberment of Riley first. Force your mother to watch the act and beg for mercy from you. Only then will you feel true freedom and release - *Posted 30 seconds ago*

Before I could finish reading Dillon's response, Mom was on the phone with Dad yelling and screaming about how now they were directing threats at me. I can't even begin to explain the rage that immersed her face as she put her cell on speaker phone so that I could hear Dad's responses. He seemed unamused and unbothered by the situation even after she repeated back the comments that were being said on SocialFriends:

"It's your daughter they're talking about now, Pete! It's your daughter!" Mom screamed.

"Rita . . . they're just empty threats behind a computer screen. Dillon's just seeking the attention; he is not going to do anything. He's just hiding behind that keyboard; you know how he is. You know him," he added.

"I know him?! I know him?! Do you know him?! Do you know your son?! Look at all the shit he's done. Look at all the crap he's doing!" she replied.

"He's putting on a show, you know that. This is what he does. Let him throw his fit; let him get it out; he'll calm down then we can discuss this entire situation with him when he's level-headed again . . . just quit feeding into it all."

"You know what? If you honestly believe that this is all going to blow over with a fucking conversation, then you have another thing coming. I'm not going to fucking sit back while he takes whatever the hell he wants from me and threatens my daughter. No Pete, that's not happening. Maybe it's time you step the fuck up and do something for once!" she cried.

"Listen—"

"I'm done listening. I'm calling the police, Pete. Do what you wish," Mom uttered.

"Enough. You're just adding to the drama and will be no better than he—"

Click. Mom hung up the phone and placed her hands over her face. The tension began to tighten her body and her arms began to shake. She let out another aggravated yell, then fell silent. I wasn't sure what to say. I was at loss for words just as she was. Dad always played "Switzerland" and tried to remain neutral through everything but this time the situation was different. The things that Dillon were doing and saying wasn't a joke anymore or something minor. He literally stole thousands of dollars from his mother. He brought a criminal—a prior California's most wanted criminal for that matter—into our house. He was describing in detail ways that he wanted to kill his mother, and now talking about killing me as well. I couldn't wrap my head around acting so nonchalantly over this. In that moment, I thought that maybe he just didn't really care. I thought he just didn't want to be bothered with us anymore but then I came to the realization that maybe he mentally just couldn't bring himself to believe what was happening. After all, if I were an outsider looking in, I'd find it all too wild to believe too. If I weren't a part of this first-handedly, I probably would have thought this was just another stunt of his as well. This was his child. Who would want to accept that their child would be capable of doing any of this? I for sure wouldn't want to come to terms with that.

After a few minutes of sitting quietly in her room, Mom picked up her cell and began dialing 9-1-1. At that exact moment, I received a text from Dad asking if she was really calling the police. I responded simply with "Yes" and directed my attention back to Mom on the phone.

"Well, that is just great. I'm on my way," he responded.

CHAPTER 15:
POLICE REPORT

It felt like ages waiting on the porch for the police to arrive. Mom sat there with her elbows resting on the glass table, supporting her face with her hands. I stayed quiet too, looking down at my phone, scrolling through the comments that were still being posted. I completely spaced out what was going on around me and was fully focused on my phone. The comments being made were just sickening, especially the ones of Dillon and Archer "celebrating" over how they were going to burn Mom into pieces. The comments just continued to go on and on and the excitement in them completely baffled me.

"Riley!" Mom mumbled while lightly hitting my leg to grab my attention. I flinched for a second then signed back in on the present. Mom casually pointed behind me. I turned and saw two police vehicles pulling into the driveway; she told me to stay quiet and to let her explain everything that was going on. I was beyond relieved to hear that I didn't have to explain it. I wouldn't have known where to start anyway.

An officer began to make his way to the porch while the other one remained in his patrol car. "Hello ma'am, I'm Officer Phillips. Did you make a call about your son and some threats?"

Mom made her way towards the entrance of the porch where the officer was waiting below with his right leg resting on the bottom step and leaning against the handrail. "Yes, that was me," she responded.

The officer nodded, glanced back at his partner who was just now exiting his car and then back towards Mom. "All right, so what's going on?" the officer asked. The second officer, Officer Colt, joined and stood next to his partner. They listened to Mom explain everything from the moment we were introduced to Damien, to the Las Vegas getaway, the money, the drugs, everything up until now when Dad's Tahoe pulled into the driveway. Mom shot me a pissed-off look as if I were the one who told him to come. It's obvious that wasn't going to be much help in this situation and most likely just added to Mom's frustration. Thankfully, my stepmom got out of the car as well. She tends to make Dad calm down if he is getting too worked up and has no problem calling him out on his shit if she feels he's wrong. *Hopefully she'll be of help here.*

The officers turned to see who was approaching. Mom explained that it was her ex-husband. Dad extended out his hand to give the officers a shake as he introduced himself: "Pete, and this is my wife, Kathy." The officer's attention drew back towards Mom, and she continued explaining what had happened. Dad stayed quiet; however, you could tell he was disagreeing. He kept looking off to the side and taking slow disappointed breaths as Mom went on. Kathy tapped his arm once or twice for him to stop and to just listen, but he was visibly getting annoyed with her as well.

"Yes, so then he came back here that next morning acting like nothing was wrong until his father questioned him on the missing money. After that, Dillon got angry, told me that he was leaving which I told him that he should. I told him he was not to take my car . . . but he did. I—"

Interrupting Mom in an attempt to lessen Dillon's actions, Dad butted in: "Uh, well, officer, the Escape is his car." Mom stared at him with a disgusted look.

"He did NOT have my permission to take MY car," she repeated sternly while staring directly into Dad's soul, sending tension amongst everyone.

"Whose name is the vehicle under ma'am?" questioned Officer Colt.

"Title, registration, and insurance are all in my name."

"All right, then it is, in fact, your car," nodded Officer Phillips.

Mom shot a sarcastic smirk before continuing with what she was saying. She finally began to explain the threats Dillon had been sending through text and posting on SocialFriends while Dad continued to roll his eyes and shake his head in displeasure. Kathy nudged him a few more times to get him to stop, but he wanted nothing to do with it. Officer Colt took notice to Dad's behavior and motioned for him to step off to the side to have a private conversation with him. The other officer asked to see the messages which Mom was more than happy to comply. She rolled back towards the table, grabbed her phone, and handed it over as officer Phillips began to scroll through the texts. His eyebrows scrunched as he shook his head, looking up from the screen. "And this is your son?" he asked. The second officer returned as officer Phillips handed over the phone to his partner for him to take a look. Officer Colt had the same facial expression as his partner and took the phone back to his car to write up a report of what was being said.

"So what happens from here, Officer?" Mom questioned.

Officer Phillips took a deep breath and exhaled stating, "Well . . . I've never seen such vulgar and disgusting language be used before towards their mother but uh, a warrant for domestic threats will be issued and as far as the car goes, it will be reported as stolen. Anyone caught driving it will be pulled over and apprehended."

"Is there a way to track where the texts are coming from? I mean, I'm concerned for his safety at this point; it's complete erratic behavior," Mom said.

"I should have asked this earlier, but does Dillon have any history of mental illness?"

"Clearly something is going on with him, but no, nothing's been diagnosed or discussed," Mom responded

"All right. And uh, no, unfortunately, we can't track where he is from the messages, but if either of you know where your son is or know anyone who knows we can go from there; until then, it's pretty much a waiting game."

Officer Phillips headed back towards his car to check up on how the report was going. The awkward tension between Mom and Dad was high as me and Kathy made eye contact with each other, signaling that neither of us knew what to say.

"Do you know where he is, Pete?" Mom boldly asked. Dad stared at her for a few seconds before responding, "No, I don't."

"Pete, what do you mean? You told me you talked to him," Kathy butted in, confused.

"No Kath, I was asking him to stop with the nonsense with his mother; he didn't tell me where he is."

"But you told me he's in Compton with Damien," Kathy persisted.

"Kath, enough. Everyone knows he's in Compton; do you know how big Compton is? Do you think I can just tell them he's in Compton and they'll magically know where he is?" he snapped back.

"Pete, if you know where he is you need to tell me," Mom chimed in.

"I don't know where he is! All he said was he was with Damien in Compton. I don't have an address and I'm also not going to throw my kid under the bus to get arrested," he replied, clearly getting frustrated.

"No, Pete! I'm not throwing my kid under any bus. I want to get him help! There is something so wrong with him and you're not doing a damn thing about it! If I could—"

"Sorry, excuse me. Here is your phone and the police report. If you hear anything else or get any more information, give us a call. We'll be in touch," Officer Colt interrupted. Mom and Dad both thanked him for his help, and the police went on their way.

"Riley, just take me inside, please. I don't want to be out here," Mom stated. I got up from my chair and opened the door so that Mom could wheel herself inside. "Thank you," she said as her voice began to crack. When I turned around, Dad was making his way up the porch with his arms extended for a hug. "All right, honey, we're going to head out. If Dillon says anything to you just ignore it please; don't feed into it." As they walked away, Kathy said something which he completely ignored, acting as if she wasn't even there. I'm surprised he didn't drive off without her.

Why is he so angry at her? Did she blow his cover? Does he actually know where Dillon is? Why is he hiding it? Why isn't he doing anything to help? Does he still think this is just a joke? Even the officer noticed his behavior and took him to the side. I wonder what story he gave, probably told him that Mom is overreacting and downplaying the situation to make Dillon look better. Maybe that's what it's about. Maybe he's afraid that Dillon's actions reflect him as a parent, and he doesn't want to carry that weight or have people judge him—or blame him. But that's true, for both Mom and Dad. They had so many chances, so many situations to step in and face that he wasn't okay, yet they did nothing about it. Or maybe this is deeper; maybe this stems back to Shane. Maybe he is afraid to recognize the situation and accept what Dillon is capable of because then it makes what happened to Shane a possible result of Dillon's rage and maybe he isn't strong enough to be faced with that. But that still doesn't make it okay; if anything, it should make this situation that much more serious for him. It should make him step up and put a stop to it. Not dance around it and play good cop, bad cop with Mom.

CHAPTER 16:
DAY FIVE

Liana came over that night to see how we were doing and if we needed anything. The three of us were in Mom's room chitchatting while the TV was playing in the background. It was nice; for those few minutes, our minds were distracted from what was going on and there were even a few laughs. But the notifications from SocialFriends continued: Dillon and Archer going back and forth, projecting ways to reach "justice" on Mom. It began taking a toll on me. The adrenaline pumping through my veins this entire time started to finally slow down and fear began to fill its place. This was my brother; we were so close growing up. We always got along, played games, drove our parents crazy with prank phone calls—you know, regular sibling things. And now? Now he's determined to kill Mom and acting like I'm just another roadblock in his way of destruction.

I was sitting on Mom's bed when tears just began pouring down my face. The energy evaporated from my body, and I fell onto the floor as my breathing increased with quick, shortened breaths.

"He's going to end up dead somewhere!" I shouted.

"Honey, no, he's not. He's going to be okay. Please calm down. Riley, please," Mom replied.

"Liana, Liana, quick, go get—go get her water! Quick! She's passing out! I'm calling an ambulance!"

It was difficult to get much rest at the hospital, not because of the uncomfortableness of the hospital bed or my inability to sleep, but because of Mom and Dad's continuous arguing. I know they thought that they were being quiet with their mumbled remarks towards each other about Dillon, but all I wanted was silence. Just a few hours of silence. But Dad kept telling Mom that she needed to calm down and to just let Dillon get his anger out because "This is how he is." Mom, of course, snipped back saying that this has gotten completely out of hand, that he needs to start realizing the seriousness of the situation.

There were two slight knocks on the open door as Dr. Stephen walked in. "Hello, Mr. and Mrs. Venturi. Riley, how are we doing?" he asked. Mom and Dad stopped arguing and greeted the doctor. I rolled off of my side and sat up in the bed. "So, this seems to be a standard anxiety attack. Your vitals have been returning to normal and we can get you ready for discharge. Now, we can also write you a script for an anti-anxiety which I feel will do you good," he added. I just wanted to get out of there and go back to my own bed. I told the doctor I didn't really want to be on any medications and that this was most likely a one-time thing. Dr. Stephen understood and handed me a pamphlet with alternative ways to decrease anxiety.

"You see, honey? You just need to relax. Stop taking everything Dillon is saying so seriously; he means nothing by it," Dad butted in.

"Stop taking it so seriously?! I've been telling you all for over a year that Dillon has been starting to scare me and acting differently! I told you last year how he was looking up how to get a hitman on Mom and you blew that off too! Now look at him! Look at what he's saying and doing!" I blurted out with anger as my heart rate began to skyrocket.

"Honey, what are you talking about? You never told me that," Dad replied.

But I did. I did tell him that. I told him that over a year ago when Dillon and I were sitting at his kitchen table with Kathy while he was standing by the stove getting dinner ready. I believe it was tacos, but don't hold me to that. Dillon was at the head of the table, I was to his right and Kathy was to his left, across from me. It was shortly after another argument between Dillon and Mom, and Kathy brought it up. One thing led to another, and I remember telling Dillon that I was afraid of him. Dillon laughed and said something like "Well you have no reason to be afraid of me." Dad actually stepped in for a moment and told Dillon that he can't tell someone how to feel which Dillon persisted on with having no accountability for. I then responded back with "You looked up a hitman on Mom—you think that's normal?"

Kathy's eyes widened, "You did what?"

"I didn't hire a hitman. I just looked up the steps on *how* to get one," Dillon defended.

"But seriously, Dillon, you think that's normal? I've been in many fights with my parents over the years and not once have I ever even thought of looking into something like that," Kathy responded.

Dad just shook his head and carried on with dinner prep.

"Well, I didn't do it. I was angry and just looked it up and afterwards, I wasn't angry anymore." Dillon laughed.

"And that's why I'm afraid of you! You now know how to get one and the next time you're mad it'll be that much easier for you to follow through!" I yelled.

Dillon started getting angry at this point and screaming at me that he has no part in how I feel and that feeling scared of him is unnecessary. I, of course, tried to yell back that he needs help and that how he reacts when he's angry isn't usual, but my yells turned into a mixture of slush with tears. Dad, like always, tried to play peacemaker and calm us down but I stormed up to the bathroom crying. Dillon grabbed his keys to leave to go back home and that was the end of that.

One would think that parents would act knowing that their child went out of their way to look up the process of ordering a hitman and where to find one, especially if it was done towards one of them and when their other child is expressing true fear because of that. Like why was that the end of that conversation? Why didn't we have a sit down with Mom after this incident? Why was this just passed off as a "This is how he is" situation? That doesn't make it okay! Kathy was more mortified over hearing about it then Dad was. Why was she the one trying to understand more and get inside of Dillon's head? Why was she the one trying to convey to Dillon that it wasn't okay or normal behavior? Why wasn't it Dad? Now he's going to stand here while I'm in the hospital and act like it's the first he's hearing of it? I expressed genuine fear back then and since then Dillon's actions have only intensified so Dad's gonna stand here and tell me that Dillon means nothing by it and is harmless when he's clearly capable of following through with every single threat he's been making? What is he so afraid of?! Why won't he finally step the fuck up and realize what his son is doing?!

Looking back on it now, that was the beginning of Dillon's real downfall. The beginning of when his anger really started to progress and become more frequent. This may have been when his drug addiction really flew into effect. I mean, that would make sense. Still, no excuse for his actions, but it makes sense. Or maybe I just want that to make sense. Maybe I just don't want to truly believe that this kind of monster has been living inside of my brother this entire time and just now getting brave enough to show itself. But it would be amazing if it were. If drugs were the sole problem here and he got into a rehab facility and overcame the addiction and got the help he needed, it would all make sense. But then again, what would be the cause of his rage and behavior while we were younger? Surely, he wasn't doing drugs as a child. I mean, I guess he could have started in middle school; that's not completely unheard of. Maybe he just didn't touch the harder stuff like meth until he was older? Or maybe this truly is who Dillon is and that this "monster" inside of him is what led to the addiction and not the other way around.

"See, honey, this is what the doctor is taking about. You need to relax; you can't get all worked up like this. I don't remember that conversation but I'm sure Dillon was just messing around. I doubt he actually was looking for a hitman."

"Whatever," I mumbled as I began to make my way out of the bed to put my shoes on. I just wanted to get out of there and to go home. I didn't want to hear any more excuses from Dad. And Mom didn't need any more of his added stress either, but unfortunately, he was our ride home.

The ride felt like it took hours, even though we lived only a few minutes from the local hospital. No one said a word; it was a tense atmosphere. Dad tried to bring up the situation with Dillon, but Mom simply put her hand up and said, "Pete, enough." And that was the end of that.

As we pulled up into the driveway there was a black four-door sedan parked in the driveway and two men in suits were standing at the front door. The two men began to make their way down the porch towards our car when they saw us pull in. One man was heavy set, with a plaid button-up under his blazer, clean shaven with a bald head. The other was thinner with glasses and a beard. Both men had badges hanging from a lanyard around their neck, the heavier-set one was carrying a clipboard while the thinner gentleman had a letter in his right hand.

"Who the hell is this now?" Mom questioned. Dad told her to wait in the car as he got out and approached the two men a few feet away from the car. Mom rolled down her window so that she could hear what was going on.

"We're looking for Dillon Venturi," the man with the glasses spoke with a stern voice.

"That's my son; he's not here right now. Is there something I can help you with?" Dad responded.

"We're from the Los Angeles County Health Department; there's a matter that we need to discuss with him," answered the same gentleman.

We couldn't hear too much after that, but Dad took the white envelope from the man with glasses and shook both of the men's hands as they got back into their car and pulled out of the driveway. Dad walked up to the opened passenger side window to tell Mom what had happened. He told her they asked if we could give Dillon the letter and to have him call them. We were all confused at this point. Why would the health department out of all people be looking for him? I was sure they were going to be detectives or something.

"Well, open it," Mom demanded.

"What? No, we can't do that, Rita," Dad sternly responded, but before he could grip onto the letter, Mom snatched it out of his hand:

"Like hell we can't."

Mom smoothly ripped open the top of the envelope, while sucking in her bottom lip and casually humming to herself with pleasure. She unfolded the crisp letter and took a few seconds to herself to read the notice. I attempted to overlook her shoulder from the backseat, though unfortunately, the print was too small to make out. She threw the letter onto the driver's seat. "Well, your son has some type of illness that he hasn't received treatment for yet. I wonder what the hell that could be," she muttered. Dad stood there shaking his head in discontentment while opening the passenger door to help Mom out of the car.

Once inside, Mom sat by the front window, sneakily peeking through the blinds to wait for Dad to pull out of the driveway and leave.

"All right, Riley, he left; hand me my phone," hurried Mom, motioning with her hand. I handed her her cell phone and asked what was going on. "I'm calling his doctor to find out what the hell this letter is about," she answered. Now I know deep down this wasn't the right thing to do; after all, Dillon was a grown adult and had the right to his privacy, but I was also extremely curious on what it could be. What could be so serious as having the county health department show up to your house with a notice and questioning your whereabouts?

"Yes, hello, Dr. Antonio, this is Rita Venturi. I'm calling regarding Dillon. We just got a visit from the health department seeking to speak with him. I was wondering if you knew what this was all about," Mom inquired.

The call wasn't on speaker phone, but Mom kept the volume up to the max to the point where one could clearly hear the other end of the conversation as if they were having a conversation directly in front of you, so I was able to overhear the other end. "I'm sorry, Rita, Dillon came down last week and requested a new HIPAA form. He removed you from the contact list."

Mom's eyes widened as she glanced over towards me. "He did? Hm, okay . . . uh, could you tell me who he listed as an informant?" she asked.

"No, I'm sorry, hon, I'm not able to say," Dr. Antonio replied.

Mom thanked Dr. Antonio for his time and hung up the phone. She sat there for a few seconds, shoulders limp, looking up towards the ceiling, shaking her head in disapproval. I could tell she felt betrayed and aggravated. Dr. Antonio had been our family doctor for over ten years and knew our family very well. She understood that he was only doing his job, but at the same time, she felt entitled as probably any parent would when it comes to the health of their child and the severity of what it could be.

But what is it? Is he dying? Is it the flu? Is it the fucking black plague? It's something so severe that he had to go down to the doctor's last week to purposefully take Mom off of his HIPAA and emergency contact? And who the hell did he put in place? Damien? It must be! Unless he put down Dad? No, that wouldn't make sense either. It most definitely has to be Damien. But why? What is he hiding?! What is it?! What—

"Riley, are you all right?" Mom asked.

I had spaced out in thought and was standing there aimlessly. "Yeah, yeah, sorry. I was just thinking," I answered.

CHAPTER 17:
HIDE AND SEEK

Strangely enough, I slept great that night. I don't even recall falling asleep. I must have knocked right out the second I made it to bed. I mean, I guess it shouldn't be a surprise, considering everything that had happened the last few days. My energy just faded out. It was the first time in what felt like forever that I had slept through the night. I probably would have slept for several more hours if Mom didn't come knocking on my door to see if I was all right, as it was already the afternoon. Although I was awake, I didn't move from bed. I stayed bundled under the covers, wrapped like a cocoon, warm and snug. I was just about to fall back to sleep when I felt a light, quick, vibration from underneath my pillow. I slid my hand under and pulled out my phone. It was a text message from Dillon's long-time friend since preschool, Jennifer.

Jennifer: Hey you, just checking in on you guys. Wanted to know if I could stop by later on. How's Mom? – *Received at 1:02 pm*

Jennifer was the only friend of his that I still trusted to this point. I've known her basically my entire life and she's one of the few "friends" not commenting on Dillon's post encouraging his insanity. I was sure Mom felt the same way; she loved Jennifer as if she were her own daughter. Always having her over for dinner, doing pickups and drop-offs when they were kids and even inviting her on family vacations, so I didn't bother asking first before I told her yes to coming over. It may do Mom some good seeing her and who knows, maybe she knows more information about everything going on that could help us.

Mom and I were in the kitchen having a simple lunch, tuna fish on potato rolls, when the front door opened. I could tell by Mom's expression that she feared it was Dillon strolling on in. I gave a quick smile and told her not to worry—it was only Jen. Her face lit up with relief and excitement and called her on over to the kitchen.

"Hi honey, what a nice surprise," Mom said as Jennifer wrapped an arm around her and bent down to give Mom a kiss on the cheek.

"I told Riley I was coming over. I hope you don't mind."

"No, not at all, sweetie. You're always welcome here."

Mom motioned for Jennifer to take a seat and told me to put up a cup of tea for them. The conversation didn't automatically start off about Dillon. They were more or less catching up on things since it had been a few months since they had last seen each other, and it was clearly doing Mom good. Her body became more relaxed, and she actually cracked a few smiles and laughs, which was a relief to see. However, after about an hour the topic did eventually come up. Jennifer held Mom's hand and asked her how she's holding up. Mom tried to crack a joke to lighten the mood; she hated people she cared about seeing her upset or stressed. She said, "Ha, well, you know, just another day in hell." Jennifer rubbed Mom's hand and assured her things were going to get better and not to worry as she's been in daily contact with Dillon trying to reason and understand what has been going through his head.

"He stole so much from me, Jen. So much money and I don't understand why," Mom shamingly said.

Jennifer took a deep breath in and exhaled, "I know he did. I asked him all of the time how he was getting money to go out with us since he didn't have a job. He'd tell us all that you would give him money since taking care of you *was* his job."

Now let's get one thing cleared up; yes, Mom often did give us money here and there when going out with friends, whether we had money or not, but it certainly was not an everyday thing. Yes, she was extremely generous and, yes, we were spoiled beyond idea growing up, but she would not have given him that much money for that amount of time. No way in hell. This also wasn't the first time I've heard him use Mom being disabled as an excuse not to work. He often liked to play the victim card with that as well. Whenever my parents would press him about looking for work or question him on what he wanted to do with his life, he would work up a story about how he's unable to work because he takes care of her. And quite frankly, Mom was getting sick of hearing that as an excuse because he was always out and about with friends, coming home at odd hours during the night and even spending days at a time in his room without seeing any of us. Now, if he really was taking care of Mom round the clock, how would any of that even be possible? Not only that, but also Mom's disability isn't even that bad. She mainly just has trouble walking and getting around due to neuropathy from diabetes. Sometimes, she may need help opening something but other than that she's good to go. This really was a rough topic for her though. I think that hurt her more than anything because all she ever tried to do our entire lives was give us everything and she always wanted to watch us succeed—Mom gave us the tools and freedom to do so. So to hear that her son constantly told people that his life was at a standstill because of her really gutted her. Maybe he honestly did believe that though and maybe he actually did view what he did for her as being a full-time job, not just something he did out of the kindness of his heart for his mother who gave him everything, but as a means to profit from in some type of way.

"Jen, that's not true. You know that's not true."

"I know, Mama. I spoke with him on the phone the other day and asked him to tell me the truth. I asked him if it was true, of him stealing money and he finally told me yes. That he would blend in withdrawals with other purchases that you would send him out for so that you wouldn't notice, or that he would take little amounts from your cabinet here and there so that it wouldn't stand out."

"But why? Why would he do that? Was it the drugs? I didn't even know he was on anything. How could I not have seen that?"

"No, no. Do *not* blame yourself here, Mama. This isn't your fault. My parents have said for years that Dillon needed help. It's him. This isn't you; this isn't Pete; and, Riley, it's not you either. I do know though that he's been doing meth for a few years, but I didn't know he had gotten this bad with it. We all used to casually smoke pot and try other things, but I didn't realize he had gotten as bad as he is." Jennifer reluctantly confessed this to Mom.

There were a few seconds of silence, not knowing what to say next, then Jennifer continued, "Can I ask you something?" She directed the question towards Mom. Mom nodded her head in agreement.

"Do *you* have a drug problem?"

Mom inhaled through her nose before exhaling and letting her shoulders go limp. "No, I do not and have never had a drug problem. That's another lie of his to gain attention."

"I'm sorry that I asked. I feel terrible for believing it. He told all of us for years now that you were highly addicted to pain medications. I even used to beg him a few times when I was in pain after my leg surgery to ask you for something, anything to help the pain and he always had an excuse as to why he couldn't get them. I thought of asking you myself, but I didn't want to overstep."

"Honey, you know if I had anything that I would have helped you. Nothing that he is saying is true."

"Jen, I have a question," I sputtered in. "Yesterday, the health department came here and handed us a letter for Dillon. It said that there's an important issue that they need to contact him about. We called his doctor, but he took Mom off as a HIPAA contact. Do you know what any of that could be about?"

Jennifer looked stuck. Like she knew the answer, like she knew what it was about but at the same time didn't want to violate his privacy. Which I understood. But also I wanted to know. I was worried about him and wanted any information at all that could help to piece together this puzzle. "Ah . . . I'm not really sure. He was saying something a while ago about wanting to get something or trying to get something, but I thought he was joking. That's the only thing that comes to mind of what it could be," she cautiously answered.

"What do you mean get something? We're just worried, like is he dying or something?" I questioned.

"No, he's not dying. Not at all. I don't really want to get in the middle of it in case that's not what it is, ya know? I don't really want to spread his business too much unless I have to."

"Yeah, I mean I get it. There's just so much going on with him and we're just so confused. It's like everything I thought I knew about him is just a lie. Do you know where he is though? Since you said you've spoken with him?"

Jennifer looked completely puzzled by that question. "Wait—what do you mean? Look . . . I really don't want to say too much. I just think you should talk with your Dad."

"Hold on, what does Pete know?" Mom asked.

"I'm sorry, I really don't want to say too much. Just talk to Peter, please. I really have to go. I'm so sorry." Jennifer got up from the chair and slightly rubbed my back before leaning down to give Mom a hug. Her complexion was pale, and she had that worrisome puppy dog look in her eyes before heading for the door.

Okay, what the hell was that about? Why wouldn't she tell us anything? We've been sitting here for days worried sick and afraid that Dillon's going to end up dead or hurt himself or us and she's just concerned about "saying too much"? I mean, I get she's Dillon's best friend and that she feels a sense of loyalty to him but c'mon! This kid's out in who the hell knows where, sending threats, getting completely out of control and she couldn't tell us anything? Evidently she knew the answers to what we were asking! And Dad? Why the fuck do I need to speak to Dad? I just saw him yesterday and he's been clueless in this all . . . unless . . . unless he's been acting clueless. But why? Why would he be letting us worry and go through all of this stress if he knew all of this information all along? What does he think he's accomplishing here?

I immediately grabbed my phone and sent a message to Dad, simply saying, "Do you know where Dillon is?" Mom and I sat at the table waiting for a response for a few minutes. Time seemed to be lagging, passing by in slow motion. Minutes seemed like hours. No response. Mom got fed up and made her way to the front door. She said she wanted to be alone for a while, but I knew exactly what that meant. She wanted a cigarette to calm her nerves and was probably going to call Dad without me hearing. Although I wanted to listen so badly, I respected her privacy and went up to my room instead of listening by the window. I mean, obviously if anything happened, she would tell me anyway, so I knew I wouldn't be missing anything.

A half hour later Mom called out for me from the front door. I figured she needed help getting back inside, but when I came down she told me to come sit outside with her. "Your father has Dillon. Picked him up last night," she said. I was in complete shock. It was after six o'clock at night and he went all day without telling us? You would think the very first person he would tell would be her. I wonder how long he would have gone without saying something if Jennifer never came over and said something.

"He has him? What did he say?"

"Said he was waiting for everything to calm down a bit before letting me know. I hung up the fucking phone."

"Well what's going to happen now? Are you letting the police know?"

"I don't know, Riley, okay?! I don't fucking know anything. I'm sick of this hide and seek game with your fucking father and brother."

CHAPTER 18:
INTERVENTION

That next morning I was awoken by Mom yelling at who I assumed was on the phone. "No, Pete! Do not let him drive that car! He'll fucking take off!"

"And if that happens, call me and I will explain it to them. He's unstable, Peter."

"I'm not going to. Can you knock this shit off already? If he doesn't go willingly, then they're being called."

After hanging up the phone, Mom made her way down the hall to my room. She told me that Dad and Kathy were on their way over, along with Dillon, for a discussion, pretty much an intervention at this point. They wanted to all sit down and get inside of Dillon's head to try to get a feeling of where his head was truly at. Apparently, Dad told Mom that Dillon doesn't understand why she's so upset with him. That he was just angry at the time and needed to get out his anger, so I'm sure this discussion is going to go *amazingly.* I was still curious though at how and why Dad had Dillon and didn't say anything to us. For all I know, he knew where Dillon was this entire time and let us go through all of that worry, stress, and fear for no reason. But at the same time, I knew this wasn't the moment to interrogate Mom on that topic and that the focus right then had to be getting to the bottom of Dillon's behavior.

A short while later, the gravel in the driveway began to shuffle and two cars pulled into the driveway: Dad's silver Tahoe, followed by the black Escape that Dillon had taken off with. "They're here," I called out to Mom. My heart sank and my chest clenched when I saw Dillon get out of the passenger seat of the Tahoe that Kathy was surprisingly driving. He had a smile on his face and a glow in his eyes as if it was just a normal, casual day. Dad got out of the Escape and motioned for Dillon to continue up the walkway to the porch. Now that phone call earlier made sense. Mom was telling Dad to drive the Escape here instead of Dillon in distress that he would back out from coming here and take off again. That was a good call on her part.

I was too nervous to stand on the porch with Mom for the initial "greeting," so I waited anxiously in the kitchen for them to come in. "Hi, Mommy," Dillon said.

There was a slight pause of what I can only imagine was an awkward silence amongst my mother and brother being face to face for the first time in a week. "Hi, Dillon," Mom awkwardly answered.

"Can I have a drink?" Dillon asked as the screen door suddenly opened, and he once again came bouncing down the hall into the kitchen like old times. I was sitting in the corner, so he didn't see me straight away. He opened the fridge and grabbed a bottle of soda. As he was closing the door to the fridge and turned around, he spotted me. He slightly jumped as if my being there startled him and let out a giggle. "Hi, Riley," he said with a smile.

"Hi," I answered, looking down at my phone. I tend to turn to my phone in anxious situations as a way to avoid what's going on. I opened up my text messages and pretended I was busy, when in reality I was just scrolling up and down on the screen. After a few seconds, the screen door opened once more and Mom, Dad, and Kathy came into the kitchen. Mom and Kathy both took a seat while Dad stood against the counter and Dillon leaned against the fridge. I stayed sitting on the stool in the corner, attempting to stay out of the conversation.

Dillon stood there with a grin on his face and cheeks fading to red. Each time eye contact was made between him and Mom, his grin grew bigger as if he was struggling to hold back laughter.

"Everything's always a joke to you," Mom firmly stated while shaking her head in disapproval and turning away.

"I don't know why you guys are so mad," Dillon responded with laughter in his voice.

"You . . . you don't know why? You have no idea at all why any of us are so upset right now?"

Dillon again let out a condescending laugh before responding "No, I don't."

"You know what—"

"Rita, Rita," Dad interrupted while putting his hand up, signaling her to stop talking.

"We're all just worried about you Dillon. We just want to make sure that you're okay," he continued.

"Well, I am fine. There is nothing to worry about. I am more than fine, I am fantastic, I am free. I am all those things and more. I am the—"

"You know what, Dillon? Get out. Just fucking get out," Mom barked, cutting Dillon off.

"All right, all right, guys, just stop. Relax," Dad interrupted.

"I don't know what her problem is," responded Dillon.

"Oh I don't know, maybe it's the threats you sent? The disgusting and sickening things you said to me?"

"Well, I was mad. You shouldn't take things so seriously."

"Buddy, you don't say those things to your mother. C'mon"

"You were mad? So that makes it okay? And what about the threats to your sister?"

Dillon glanced over towards my direction. I immediately looked down to break the eye contact. I didn't want any part of this conversation. My chest was tightening, and it felt as if it were a hundred degrees in the room. I didn't know what to do anymore. After everything that he said and did, he was standing there clueless. I couldn't tell if he was making jokes of it or if he really didn't see anything wrong with what he did. I'm not sure any of us knew and quite frankly, I'm not sure which scenario is worse.

"No one was going to do anything to her. She shouldn't have gotten involved when nothing concerned her," he responded while taking a sip of his soda. Mom and Dad sort of just looked at each other as if they were communicating telepathically and sighed.

"Okay, Dillon. And what about the stealing?" Mom questioned.

"What stealing?"

"The stealing! The money, the cameras, the jewelry, the stealing!"

"If you view it as stealing, then that's on you. I haven't stolen anything and that's all I have to say on that."

Mom cupped her head into her hands; her body began to tense as she let out a frustrated, helpless yell from not having anything else to say. Kathy softly patted and rubbed Mom on the back of her shoulders.

"Buddy, are you going to answer any of these questions? Or is this just going to be a waste of time?" Dad asked.

"I am answering. Just because I'm not answering in the format or the way that you created to yourself doesn't mean that I'm not answering. I love questions. I love jeopardy. Ask away, Daddy-o"

"Dillon, we're not joking here. This is serious. Dad sighed before continuing on. "Your drug addiction—how long has that been going on for?"

"I don't have an addiction."

Kathy and I locked eyes in surprise by that response. I think that response was the most shocking one of all up to that point. Dad even looked thrown off guard. To be honest, I had to hold back a laugh when I heard that. You know those situations where something is just so ridiculous that it turns into being humorous? Well, yeah, that was definitely it. The way that sentence so firmly and easily flew from his lips without any hesitation or thought—he was actually being serious. He openly believed what he just said.

"What . . . what . . .?"

"What was found in my room was a collection over the course of the last three years. I am a drug user. I am not a drug addict," Dillon continued, this time with a sly smirk reemerging.

Dad shook his head and rolled his eyes in annoyance. He seemed to finally be starting to grasp the fact that Dillon really was in need of help and that he actually wasn't comprehending the seriousness of this situation. Up until this point, Dad had kept a pretty neutral face. He was cautious not to let his emotions bleed through in an effort to keep the conversation calm and successful instead of it turning into a screaming and blaming match. But now, his facial muscles began to tighten, and redness began seeping into his face. He stood there for a few seconds with his arms crossed over his chest, his right arm slanted upward holding his chin between his thumb and pointer finger staring at Dillon.

Dillon stared back and let out another laugh. "What?"

"Why'd you steal your passport?" Dad questioned, still firmly holding his stancc and cyc contact.

"I didn't steal it; it belongs to me. I took what was mine"

"Then why did you take it? What need did it have?"

"Don't ask questions you don't want the answer to," Dillon coldly answered.

"What is that supposed to mean? Buddy, I want to know"

"It means what it means. Don't ask me those kinds of questions."

"Dillon, why did you need your passport?" he asked again while nudging Dillon with his eyes, as if he knew something already that we didn't.

"Don't worry about it. Oh, by the way—the high hits quicker if you inject it through your ass."

"Dammnit, Dillon! This isn't a fucking game!" Mom scolded while slamming her fist down onto the table, causing the coffee in the mug to spill over. Kathy jumped up and grabbed a stack of napkins that were on the table and began to soak up the coffee while Mom and Dad just stared blankly at nothing.

"Look, Dill, we all just care about you, okay? We're all here because we're worried about you and this guy that you're with is going to get you into trouble," Kathy softly expressed.

"That's fine. I love him."

"You love him? Do you think he's going to love you when you're in jail?" Dad said.

Dillon's eyes began to brighten with excitement as if he just thought of a way to end world hunger or something big. "We'll go to jail together. It'll be perfect!" he responded.

"You think they're going to put you two together? That they'll put you two in the same cell and let you play house all "lovey-dovey," like it's a damn vacation? Buddy, I'm done here."

Dillon's facial expression said it all. His eyebrows raised, eyes widened, and mouth opened. He was surprised, shocked even, that Dad just read his mind and recited word from word precisely what he was thinking or envisioning in his head. He stood there stunned; paranoia was definitely zig-zagging through his mind, questioning who else could read his thoughts. It was comical in a sense, like a scene from a scripted sitcom. You know, there's always that one character who's a little bit on the slower side not picking up on sarcasm and such while the camera pans in and you hear the laughter overplay from the audience . . . only we were still waiting on the cue to laugh.

"We want you to go get a psychological evaluation," Mom softly spoke as if she were too drained to pocket enough oxygen to speak. She didn't even glance towards Dillon's direction. She kept her stare straight ahead towards the window. I kept my attention on my phone, acting in such that I wasn't paying any mind to the conversation so that I could continue to stay out of it; however, I began to record the conversation. I'm not sure why I decided to record or why at that particular moment, but I did. Looking back, maybe I sensed things were about to go sour, maybe I had an urge to record in case anything happened there would be proof, or maybe I just simply wanted it for my own selfish reasoning like sending it to my friends or looking back on it to tell the story. This story.

The energy in the room suddenly became heavy and darkened. I glanced up from my phone to see Dillon flash to red, muscles tightening, eyebrows diving inward and eyes scrunching as he began slowly making his way towards Mom with his pointer finger firmly extended at her. He took slow steps until his finger was inches from touching the side of her face while uttering through his teeth; "For what reason? I am in the clearest and healthiest place mentally that I have ever been in my entire life. I have let go of living to please others and because I do not serve you any longer, you have created the illusion in your own head that there must be something wrong with me. Instead of coming to terms to accept that I have broken free from the bars you have put around me, you live in a fantasy of *oh poor little Rita and her clinically insane son!*"

"Buddy, back off of your mother," Dad responded, matching Dillon's tone.

"Either you go voluntarily to the hospital and check yourself in, or I will contact the police and let them know that you are here, and they WILL come. They WILL arrest you and they WILL put you in for an evaluation whether you want it or not," Mom answered while keeping her glare fixed at the window.

"Ha-ha, okay. Let's go. I love games. I can fool them. Oh, Dillon can fool anyone and everyone."

Why is he talking about himself in the third person all of a sudden? Am I the only one who picked up on that? Am I the only one who finds that strange? He goes from being in flames to skipping jolly out of the house as if the psych hospital is a fucking field trip in a matter of seconds! Is he playing a game? Is he serious? Is he actually finding this humorous? I'm so sick of this! How can he stand there with no empathy for Mom and manipulate everything to make it sound like she's the crazy one? Like she's the one in the wrong! Like he's done nothing ill here! Is he acting? Is he playing the part? The way his emotions and body language go from calm to enraged with a simple blink, is he—I—I don't even know what I'm saying anymore. And Mom, she looks so helpless. She has no energy left; she's broken. She just sat there staring defeated out the window. She didn't even flinch when he walked up to her and the way he stood over her and bent down to her ear when speaking, she didn't care. She sat blank, emotionless as if she didn't care what he did to her. Why does he hold so much power over us? Why are we so scared of him? Why did I stay quiet? Why didn't I speak up? Maybe I'm to blame for this as well. Maybe it's not just all on Mom and Dad, but he's not my kid. It's not my responsibility to steer him the right way in life and throw down the hammer. But maybe I shouldn't have stayed quiet either.

CHAPTER 19:
INTAKE: PART 1

Dillon bounced out of the kitchen, skipping down the hallway to the front door. The rest of us in the room shot stares amongst each other with looks of "*What the hell just happened?*" written on our faces. I let a subtle smirk appear for a few seconds from the awkwardness that floated through the room but that quickly suppressed once eye contact was made with Mom.

"Hello-o-o, are we going, my loves? Dillon doesn't like to wait." Dillon's light flirtatious tone traveled through the house causing goosebumps across my arms.

Mom and Dad looked at each other, waiting for the other one to speak first. "I don't want to ride with him," Mom mouthed to Dad, who nodded his head in agreement.

"Pete, how about you ride with Dillon in Rita's car? I'll follow behind with her and Riley," Kathy suggested. Dad nodded once more and headed out of the kitchen towards Dillon. "C'mon buddy, it's you and me."

Kathy and I helped Mom stand up and take a hold of her walker. We slugged behind Dad and Dillon. Kathy walked ahead of us while I stood closely behind Mom in case she were to lose her balance, or maybe I trailed behind because I anxiously didn't want to go and be dragged into this nonsense. By the time we made it onto the porch, Dad was already in the driver's seat of Mom's Explorer with his elbow resting on the side of the door, hand folded into a fist which his forehead was leaning against. That was the first time throughout this situation that I had seen him look worn as well. Perhaps he felt this way all along but was just better at hiding it than Mom or maybe he felt that he had to keep strong in front of us. Then again, maybe he was just annoyed and wanted nothing more to do with any of this.

Meanwhile, there was Dillon dancing seductively against the rear of the car, twerking against it with his cigarette smoking from his lips. "He's a fucking idiot," Mom whispered to herself while I assisted her down the steps of the porch.

Dad looked up and made eye contact with Kathy, sharing a look of disapproval before rolling down the window. "Dillon, get in the damn car."

"Coming, Daddy," he responded while softly flicking his cigarette onto the gravel, giggling, and skipping to the passenger-side door. By this time the three of us were passing behind the Explorer towards Dad's Tahoe. Mom and Kathy kept their glare straight ahead as they passed Dillon, but I couldn't control my urge to look at him. I could feel his stare gleaming onto my skin like rays of the sun firing down onto the sand. He was standing there with his left hand on the handle of the door with his head turned to the side following us with his eyes. Waiting for someone to look his way. To acknowledge him. I slowly glanced towards him and locked senses as he flashed a soothing smile, giving a playful wink before opening the door and getting into the car.

For those few seconds, I felt an almost calm feeling fill my lungs, which I realize is strange considering the position. But that smile was just so charming and light, I felt safe in a way. It was like we were little kids again, taking walks to the gas station, playing for hours in our yard, building tents in the living room out of blankets and filling it with snacks. There was my brother. He was right there. Then the slam of the door. I blinked and shook it off.

How does he do that? How does he switch on and off like that? Was that him? Was that really him? Or was that him "fooling" me for those split seconds like he said he could? Was he getting into the "zone"? Putting on that "sparkling charm"? Preparing for his lead role in escaping the psychiatric ward?

"Riley, seatbelt," Mom muttered. I zoned back in, buckled up and just like that we were on the road, following cautiously behind Dad and Dillon. The first few minutes were still and lifeless. I can't speak for Mom or for Kathy, but my mind was spinning. Different scenarios of what would happen and follow flashed through like hazard lights on a car.

This is it! It's finally happening! This circus show is finally coming to an end! He'll get the help he needs; he'll be okay. He'll be my brother again. They'll see right through his act! I mean, they will, right? They're doctors. Professionals. They probably see this kind of thing all the time. They'll call his bluff . . . or . . . what if they don't? What if he's truly that good of an actor? What if he's mastered this game? What if he walks on in there through those hospital doors and they think we're the crazy ones? What happens then? What if this just triggers him even more? What if he comes out bleeding revenge?

"Jesus Christ! This kid never fucking stops!" Mom shouted.

"Is he for real?" Kathy questioned.

I sat up straight and peeked my head between the middle of the two front seats to get a view of what was going on ahead. Dillon's legs were going in and out of the passenger side window in a bicycle motion as if he was on a slow stroll through the neighborhood. He had to have been leaning his back against Dad's side in order to be able to do what he was doing. I can only imagine Dad's reaction. He was probably sitting there keeping his focus on the road, firmly shaking his head, and grinding his teeth. After a few seconds the legs out of the window stopped, only to be greeted with his head popping up and down out of the moon roof of the Explorer like he was a mole in that carnival game whack a mole, where the objective is to try to hit the little moles that pop up out of the hole before they go back down. But just like the legs out of the window, the head pops halted just as quickly. He probably got elbowed by Dad and told to "knock it off already" like he always would when we would act up in the car as kids.

One of our favorite things to do when we were younger was to bother Dad. I'm not sure why we thought it was so funny to aggravate him so much, but we did. Especially when we were in the car. The two of us would throw candy and food out of our windows and take turns to see who would get caught first. When he would go into stores we would hold the horn down for minutes at a time or to the tune of certain well-known songs like "Twinkle, Twinkle, Little Star" and he would come out from the store fuming! His face would be red and serious; he'd aggressively get into the car and slam the door before yelling at us: "Knock this shit off!" The best part was when he would back out of the parking spot to find all of the trash from his car lying there in the parking lot. Dillon and I would open the car doors and shove all of his trash underneath the car so that when he pulled out he would see a litter of garbage consume his spot. We thought it was the most hilarious thing ever. Dad would then become very heavy on the gas and brake pedals and take turns like it was a race track. The harder we laughed, the madder he became. I think it was the veins that would pop out from his forehead and neck that made it so funny. I mean, we were kids; we thought he looked amusing.

Dillon even had a habit when we were young to pop out from Dad's sunroof or windows while in drive-thrus, just screaming on the top of his lungs. People would become startled thinking that someone was being murdered or kidnapped or something. His screams would cut through the ears and cause everyone to stop in their tracks. Dad would start nudging Dillon with his elbow telling him to "get the fuck in the car." At the time, I thought it was hysterical. I would even egg him on: *"Dillon, do the thing,"* and he would. But that behavior should have ended there. We were kids doing silly, harmless, things. But to be nearing your thirties now continuing the behavior, and in such a serious situation, something's just not right there. It wasn't funny anymore. Though, to passing cars, I'm sure it looked humorous. I saw a few people smirk while going by, thinking it was just someone having fun and messing around, not knowing the background to the condition. But it wasn't funny.

We finally pulled into the parking garage of the hospital and parked alongside Dad and Dillon. Dad got out of the car and walked over to Kathy's window to talk to her and Mom. They were discussing how they wanted to proceed and making sure everyone was ready when once again the moon roof of the Explorer slid open and out crawled Dillon. This time he climbed completely out and went on all fours, like a dog, on the roof. He began moving his body up and down almost as if he was humping the air underneath him while Brittney Spears' song "Toxic" played from his phone. The three of us unanimously turned our heads and watched the scene unfold. Once Dillon realized he had our attention, he slid down the windshield from the roof and spread out across the hood of the car. He began convulsing while yelling, "Look Mommy! I'm playing the part! I'm playing the part!" His voice rebounded through the parking garage as people began to stare.

"Let's go. Now." Dad sternly demanded while snapping his fingers at him and pointing towards the entrance of the hospital.

"He-he-he," Dillon giggled while he jumped down from the hood and softly skipped towards the door. Dad followed behind.

I got the walker from the trunk and Kathy assisted me in helping Mom stand and grab hold of it. Mom joked and suggested the three of us leave Dad and Dillon here on their own. We all smiled, knowing that would turn out to be a disaster. As we headed towards the entrance after them, I realized that music was still playing even though Dad and Dillon were already inside. "Hold on," I instructed as I hurriedly walked back towards our cars. There I spotted Dillons phone in the indent of where the windshield and hood of the car met and picked it up. His phone must have pushed out from his back pocket when he slid down the windshield and not noticed. I shut the music off and made my way back to Mom and Kathy. "He left this." I extended the phone out towards Mom who took it and placed it in the seat of her walker.

Upon entering, I heard Dillon call my name. "Over here, Riley! I saved you a seat!" I glanced to my right and there he was waving at my direction with a huge smile stretched across his face. Dad was standing against the wall, arms crossed. Mom and Kathy found seats diagonal from them, and I dreadfully made my way over towards Dillon and sat down.

"So who's going to check me in? Mommy? Would you like to do the honors?" Dillon asked in a joking manner.

"No, Dillon. You have to check yourself in," Mom responded short and to the point.

"Hm, okay!" Dillon shrugged his shoulders and rose from his seat. He confidently walked up to the desk, placed both palms of his hands onto the counter and laughingly stated: "I'm here for a psych evaluation."

The young receptionist looked the furthest from pleased. "For whom?" she asked.

"For me!" he answered louder, projecting his voice for the packed waiting room to hear. The room was close to silent up to this point. Everyone seemed to either have the same emotionless look or the worrisome anticipation waiting for answers expression on their faces. The last thing any of them were wanting to hear was a scene from Dillon checking himself into the psychiatric ward.

"Are you suicidal or wanting to harm others?" the receptionist questioned.

Dillon began to grin as he stepped to the side and motioned his arm outwards towards Mom as if he was leading up to a surprise.

"This woman right here. That's right, Mommy—don't look away! This is what you wanted, wasn't it? The attention and sympathy from others of having a child who's clinically insane, right? Well, this woman right here—she thinks I'm crazy and being the supportive son that I am,

I'm honoring her wishes for an evaluation. Where do I sign up?"

The receptionist's eyes widened and shot a look of irritation towards Mom then quickly back towards Dillon.

"May I have your name?" she asked while handing Dillon a clipboard with paperwork to complete. Dillon lit up like this was the moment that he was waiting for.

"Dillon. Dillon Venturi," he arrogantly pronounced while giving a patronizing wink and walking back towards his seat, flashing the clipboard in Mom's direction like it was something to be proud of. Like it was a damn diploma or something.

He sat there with his legs crossed, tapping the blue ball-point pen against the clipboard, giggling as he filled out the paperwork. People seated around him gave quick glares every now and then, looking away when he would glance up. He caught one lady staring; he gave a stretched grin and waved with his fingers wiggling back and forth. She instantly looked down, fidgeting with her phone to break the interaction. I don't blame her. I would—I *do*—do the same thing. Kathy, however, kept her stare sealed on him the entire time. She looked confused and amazed by him all at once. She was fascinated with what she was seeing, like she couldn't believe how he was acting, only breaking her gaze for a few seconds at a time to peek at me or to see how we were reacting. Like usual, Dad just stood there, arms crossed, looking straight ahead, avoiding eye contact with any of us.

"Mommy, do you have a dollar? I want some chips from the machine," Dillon asked, breaking the hushed friction amongst us.

Mom let out a slight laugh, but it wasn't the *"that's-so-funny"* kind of laugh, it was the *"did he-really-just-ask-me-that?"* kind of laugh. She started to dig her hand into her pocket when Dad extended out a few dollars towards Dillon, beating her to it. "Here," he said.

"He-he, thank you!" Dillon responded. He placed the clipboard down on his chair and casually walked up to the vending machine before looking back and asking if I wanted anything, to which I shook my head no.

While he was occupied scanning the vending machine for which snack he wanted, I looked down at the clipboard and couldn't help but think *"What the fuck?"* Dillon's answers to every question was "sex." It asked for his name, he wrote "sex." Asked for his birthday, he wrote "sex." Asked for medical information and insurance, he wrote "sex." Emergency contact person, yep, he put "sex." Dillon came back after a few minutes with four bags of chips in his hand, picked up the clipboard and plopped down into his seat.

"Are you finished filling that out?" Mom questioned.

"Yep. All done, Mommy," he answered mockingly.

"Go hand it in then."

"Riley, can you hold my chips for me?"

"Yeah, no problem," I answered.

He walked back up to the counter and handed the clipboard to the receptionist. When she took the clipboard, she glimpsed down at the forms and a puzzled look appeared. She looked up for a second at him like she was waiting for a camera crew to come out telling her she's on one of those hidden-camera television shows where they pull outrageous pranks on people.

"You can take a seat. We'll call you when we're ready."

Dillon made his way back to his seat and I handed him his bags of chips.

"Are you sure you don't want any?" he asked again.

"No, I'm okay. Thank you," I replied.

Dillon sat there crinkling the bags on his lap, quietly laughing to himself under his breath. He knew what he was doing. He was trying to irritate Mom. Sounds such as crinkling bags or loud chewing always infuriated her. I could tell she was trying her hardest to ignore him, but that only caused him to progressively crinkle louder.

"Dillon," Dad firmly spoke while putting his palm up to gesture for Dillon to stop. Thankfully, he stopped him before Mom exploded. I could tell it was taking everything in her not to snap from the noise.

Another minute or two passed when Dillon suddenly ripped open the bag of cheese doodles and shoved the entire contents of the bag into his mouth and started laughing. The chips filled his cheeks, expanding them like a puffer fish. I'm surprised he didn't dislocate his jaw with how wide his mouth hung open. No one else in that room was entertained besides him. I tried my best not to smile because Dillon definitely would have taken it as a confirmation smile that what he was doing was funny, when in actuality, it was due to pure embarrassment. I couldn't help it though. I smiled and laughed, needing to turn away so that he wouldn't see me and take it as a cue to continue. Every time he laughed or chomped down, chips would crumble out of his mouth and fall onto his lap. He then opened the next bag and struggled to fit more. At this point he was just basically smashing chips against his lips as they were crushing out from under his hand, sprinkling down his shirt and piling onto his thighs since his mouth could fit no more.

Once Dillon went for the third bag of chips, Dad reached over and yanked it from his hand along with the fourth bag. "Enough already, dammit," he angrily muttered, which only caused Dillon to laugh louder with chips bursting from his mouth and shooting through the air before landing onto the floor.

"Just sit there and be fucking quiet," he continued, as his vein began to bulge out of his neck. And that's exactly what Dillon did for the remainder of the time in the waiting room. He sat there quietly, slowly chewing what was left of the chips in his mouth and giggling softly amongst himself.

"Dillon Venturi," a male's voice called out from the doors next to the receptionist's desk. There stood a slim, average-height man in a white coat and navy scrubs underneath accompanied by two other men in white scrubs. A pile of crumbs fell from Dillon's body as he stood up and there was a crunch under his feet as he walked towards them. He laughed once more as he said "Sorry, I was hungry," but this time his laugh was different. It wasn't the obnoxious giggles or condescending laughs like previous; it was a shorter, more awkward laughter. He was nervous. It was an untainted, nervous laugh.

A few minutes later a nurse came out and escorted us to a different waiting room in the psychiatric wing of the hospital. It was an eerie scene walking down those narrow hallways with the florescent lights beaming down. I always thought movies exaggerated psychiatric centers with the bars covering the windows on the doors and patients walking around in white gowns like medicated zombies, but they weren't exaggerations. As we passed by doors, we heard groans and yells, patients peeking out from behind the door windows and even caught a glimpse of a patient being restrained on a stretcher. This was not a place I wanted to be and knowing that Dillon was somewhere within these walls made me extremely uneasy.

The psychiatric waiting room was set up almost like a therapist's office. It was definitely more welcoming than the emergency room. The floor was finished with carpet instead of hard tile, there were soft couches instead of plastic chairs and a tv mounted on the wall with the news, a little snack nook that had a few bags of chips and fruit alongside a mini fridge filled with waters, soda cans, and even a counter for coffee. We were the only ones in there too, which was relieving; I could stretch out and relax.

"Pete," said Mom.

Dad looked in her direction and raised his eyebrows while he was slugged on the couch with his elbow leaning on the armrest and fist over his mouth, holding his head up. "Hm?" he answered.

"You want to tell me how he ended up back with you? Or are we just going to avoid that whole situation?" she sarcastically questioned.

Dad let out an irritated sigh and shook his head in bother. "Right now? Really?"

"Yes, Peter. Really."

CHAPTER 20:
DADDY TO THE RESCUE

Dillon: Daddy - *Received at 1:32am*

Dillon: Daddy, please. Please come get me. I need to leave here! - *Received at 1:33am*

Dillon: I need to leave right now - *Received at 1:34am*

Dad: Buddy, what's going on? - *Delivered at 1:35am*

Dillon: I need to leave right now - *Received at 1:35am*

Dillon: Damien and I broke up. I need to leave right now! - *Received at 1:37am*

Dad: Where are you? Where's the car? - *Delivered at 1:38am*

Dillon: I'm on the curb. Please, please. I need to leave - *Received at 1:38am*

Dad: It's after one in the morning; why are you on the curb? Buddy, you need to wait inside. Where's your car? - *Delivered at 1:40am*

Dillon: COME GET ME! - *Received at 1:40am*

"Babe, what are you doing? Go back to sleep," Kathy muffled while releasing a yawn and rolling over in bed towards Dad.

"I have to get Dillon," he quietly answered, sitting up out of bed and slipping on his shoes.

"What? Is he okay?"

"I don't know; he's just texting me that they had a fight and I have to go get him."

"A fight? Now? He can't wait? Why—"

"I don't know! I don't know, Kath, okay? I have to go. I have to get him; where's my fucking wallet?" he angrily answered as he shuffled through the darkened room scanning for his wallet, which he found on the ledge of the dresser and walked out of the door.

By the time he pulled up to Dillon's location it was well into two in the morning. Dillon was on the corner of the street in front of a brick apartment building, sliding his back up and down against a utility pole like he was a pole dancer. Dad pulled up behind him and parked at the curb. The brightness from the headlights must have startled him because Dillon jumped in shock as he turned around to see who was pulling up so late. Once he realized it was Dad, he patted his chest while letting out a breath of relief and lightly made his way over to the car.

"He-he, thank you," he said as he opened the passenger side door and got in.

However, Dad just sat there looking at him, not saying a word. Watching him. Waiting for an explanation of what's going on.

"What?" Dillon asked jokingly.

"What the hell is going on? What happened?" Dad asked.

Dillon sat there seemingly clueless before answering. "Nothing, we got into an argument. I just need a break for a day or two."

"No, buddy. What's going on? Where's your car? Where's all of your mother's things?"

"They're in his apartment; he won't give them to me."

"Which apartment is his?"

"Daddy, don't worry about it."

"Which apartment is his?" he asked again, this time more sternly.

"Just leave it alone!"

"No, Dillon! That's not the way it works! That's a lot of money the two of you took from your mother. Now tell me which apartment is his! I'm going up."

"Daddy, please! Just leave it alone. Please don't go up there. He's killed people before. He has knives. Please just leave it alone," Dillon pleaded.

That comment threw Dad off guard. He definitely wasn't expecting that to come out of his son's mouth. He stuttered over his response before taking a moment to pause—I guess to regain his train of thought. Anger consumed his face; his body clenched as he spoke through his teeth, "Get the damn car."

"He won't tell me."

"Get the car. Or I'll just call the police."

Dillon's eyes rose and doubled in size. "Okay, okay," he quickly interrupted and made his way back into the brick building. A few minutes passed before Dillon came walking out of the building, dangling the keys to the car between his fingers and flashing them in Dad's face.

"Well . . . where is it?"

"South Park," Dillon answered, slightly amused.

"What the hell is it doing there?"

"Do you want to get it or not?"

"Where's the other stuff?" Dad asked, ignoring Dillon's smart remark.

They stood there for a minute or two going back and forth about Mom's stolen items. Dillon continued to re-iterate to leave the situation alone and that it was too dangerous for him to go up to Damien's apartment. Dillon also claimed that most of the things that they had took had already been sold. After realizing arguing with Dillon was getting nowhere, Dad gave up and told Dillon to get into the car. Dad typed the address that Damien had given Dillon for the location of the car into the GPS on his phone and looked at Dillon in annoyance.

"What? Stop looking at me like that," Dillon nervously said with a soft chuckle.

"It's forty minutes from here. That's what," Dad responded.

Dad sharply pulled off from the curb and headed down the lifeless road. Dillon went to turn the radio on, but was stopped immediately by Dad, who slapped his hand off of the knob. The car was silent. Well, until it wasn't.

"Why are you mad at me?" questioned Dillon.

Dad took a deep breath in as if he was trying to calm his emotions before answering. "Why do you think, Dillon? It's after three o'clock in the fucking morning; your mother's been down my throat, your sister's terrified, we're on a scavenger hunt for this damn car, which, if by the way, isn't here, I'm going back to that apartment and handling this myself. All the while, you seem to be completely impractical about your actions and appear to believe nothing has consequences. That's why. That's why I'm mad. I can't let this one go."

Dillon sat there staring at him with an astonished and almost offended look on his face, like he was shocked that Dad wasn't brushing it off as usual. "She got to you," he replied, referring to Mom as he directed his attention back towards the road, reclining his chair. "Wo-o-ow," he mumbled under his breath just loud enough for Dad to hear.

"No. No one fucking got to me. You fucking got to me!" Dad exclaimed.

In six hundred feet, your destination will be on the right, the GPS chimed in, breaking the tension that filled the car. Dad spotted the Escape that was abandoned just shy of the street light and pulled up behind it. There was an eerie shadow that gloomed over from the light.

"Listen, Dillon. The car is reported stolen; if you get pulled over, there's nothing I can do to help you. Just slowly follow behind me and take it easy. All right? I'm not joking."

Dillon glanced to the floor nervously and begin to fidget with his fingers. "Did you hear me?" Dad asked. Still, no response. "Dillon?" he repeated.

"I'm afraid," Dillon uttered.

"Afraid of what? If you just follow behind, you'll be fine"

"No. I'm afraid that . . . that there's blood in the car."

"Blood? Why the hell would there be blood in the car?"

"I don't . . . I don't know," answered Dillon, still keeping his stare locked down at his feet, squeezing his fingers.

"Dillon. What the hell does that mean?" questioned Dad, his frustration growing.

"Damien took the car to a farm and came back without it."

"A farm? Okay, did he hit an animal?"

"No."

"What? What, Dillon? What?"

"Something shady. Trying, trying to get us out of here. Just please don't ask questions."

Dad sat there for a few seconds in silence, not sure if he was being serious or just having one of those Dillon moments where he says outrageous things as a sick joke. He grabbed the keys to the Escape, stumbled taking his seat belt off, and hurried out of the car. Dillon stayed put and watched as Dad swung open the driver's side door, took a quick glance then moved to the back door to do the same before making his way back towards Dillon.

"The car's fine," he spoke as he opened his passenger door for Dillon to get out, in which Dillon's response was just a hesitant gaze.

"There's nothing in the car. Let's go," he repeated, motioning with his hand for Dillon to get up.

Subtly unbuckling his seat belt and reaching down to grab his backpack that he had placed by his feet, Dillon stepped out of the car and stood facing Dad as a jumpy smirk bled through.

"Jesus, Dillon, this isn't a joke. Take something serious for once, would you?"

"What do you mean?" Dillon answered through laughter.

Dad stood there once again for a second staring at him with rising disappointment across his face. "Just drive carefully, all right? And follow me."

Dillon slugged towards his car and eased open the door, as if something wasn't adding up correctly—like he was shocked that the car was fine. Dad's focus remained locked on Dillon the entire time until he was fully inside of the car, probably to make sure he didn't try to make a run for it or do something stupid like he was known to do. Once fully inside, Dad got into his, pulled up alongside next to Dillon and rolled down the window. "Just follow behind me," he instructed.

The first few minutes into the ride were dull and seemed to drag on. Dad battered his eyes not to doze off, which was difficult to do at that hour when no one's with you to keep you awake. Every minute or two he would glance up at his rearview mirror to make sure that Dillon was still behind him, which he was. Well . . . you guessed it—until he wasn't. The next thing Dad knew, music blasting emerged next to him on his left-hand side and as he turned to look out his window, he locked eyes with Dillon, who gave an excited smile and waved before accelerating and taking lead, leaving Dad dragging behind.

"Jesus Christ! This kid!" Dad yelled while slamming his fist down onto the steering wheel. Dillon began swerving through the traffic lanes going in and out, back and forth, blasting Brittney Spears's song "Circus" while rotating between wrangling his arms out of the window to the rhythm of the music and sticking his head out, shouting along to the lyrics like he was in his own little world. The music was so loud that the vibrations from the song echoed throughout the body of the car, causing the windows to visually shake. Dad stayed a distance behind, waiting, secretly hoping, for a cop to spot the chaos and pull him over to put an end to this. That way, at the very least, he'd be safe. But we all know things don't happen the way we wish and that he was never pulled over. Thankfully the roads were bare at that hour, and no one got hurt.

CHAPTER 21:
INTAKE: PART 2

I wish there were words to describe the look that painted Mom's face after hearing that story of Dillon. I could tell a part of her wished she had never asked. It only added to the distress she already felt. Mom shook her head and looked away from Dad.

"Riley, can I have a water please?" she muffled in a whisper.

"Yeah, of course," I replied, getting up off the sofa towards the mini fridge and snack bar in the corner of the room.

Kathy was still glaring at Dad, mouth opened, utterly stunned at what she just heard. It was as if this was the first time even she was hearing of it. "*Blood*? Pete, you didn't tell me that," she eagerly spoke while peeping towards me, widening her eyes in an attempt to signal me to press for more information about it.

"He was just being an ass, Kath. There wasn't blood." He snickered.

But was it? Was it really him being an ass? Why else would the car be abandoned a half an hour away if there weren't some truth to that story? That's the second time now that Dillon's made a comment about them trying to get out of the country, but why?! Did they actually do something warranting their need to leave? This just isn't adding up. And then he said Damien's killed people before?! Why isn't anyone back tracking to that comment? HE'S KILLED PEOPLE?! Why didn't Dad just call the police once he got to Damien's apartment? I get not wanting your son to go to jail but like there was an opportunity right there to stop all of this bullshit!

Two hours went by while we waited for an update. The four of us sat there quietly. With his arms crossed, Dad kept his eyes locked on the television that was mounted to the wall. I highly doubt he was even paying mind to the news stories that were being broadcasted, but just kept his attention to the screen to avoid any more conversation or arguments. Mom had her focus down on her phone, scrolling with her pointer finger through what looked to be SocialFriends. Every few minutes she'd shake her head slightly in disapproval while letting out an exhausted sigh. My bets were that she was reading through the harassing comments on Dillon's status that read "Hey guys, I'm on my way to the mental institution LOL!" He posted the status during the drive to the hospital; I just hadn't brought it up then because there was enough going on as is. Mom didn't need to be bothered any more than she already was. The responses were pretty much the same genre as the ones on his post a few days ago. Some were cheering him on and wishing him luck, while others continued with threatening remarks such as a comment from Archer: "Now when you burn that bitch to crumbs, you can plead insanity!"

"Mr. and Mrs. Venturi?" a familiar voice spoke as the pale, wooden door opened. There stood the same man in the navy scrubs and white coat that escorted Dillon earlier from the waiting room. This time he was close enough for me to make out the writing on his coat. It read *DR. PETERSON PSY.D.*. "Would you mind coming with me?" he asked, holding a clipboard and motioning towards the door. Dad rose from the couch and assisted Mom with standing until she was positioned with her walker. Neither of them spoke, though Kathy and I knew to stay where we were. Mom and Dad shamefully walked out of the room, Dr. Peterson following behind.

They were led down the narrow white hall and into Dr. Peterson's office. He gestured to the two mahogany wooden chairs for Mom and Dad to take a seat. Dr. Peterson quietly closed the door behind them and made his way over to his desk as he softly pulled out his swivel chair and sat down behind his desk. The office was pretty plain and simple—

except for a bookshelf on the back left wall behind Dr. Peterson that seemed to be a mixture of thesauruses and psychology medical journals; a large metal filing cabinet sat to the right next to a window with a view overlooking the hospital's garden area. The room was fairly small, but the natural light coming in from the window helped with the illusion of a larger space. His desk was cluttered. An organized clutter, with stacks of paper, a holder for office supplies which was filled with pens and highlighters and two photo frames which were facing his direction that I'm going to assume were of his family or loved ones since that's what most people tend to display at work.

Dr. Peterson looked down at his clipboard and flipped through a few pages, which were mirrored through the reflection of the gloss finish that coated his wooden desk. "So, Dillon is your son, correct?"

"Yes," Mom and Dad spoke in unison. Dad had his arms crossed with his left hand resting in the crease of his elbow of his right arm, as his right arm was pointed upward holding his chin between his thumb and pointer finger like he was in deep thought or something. Mom was more slumped in the chair dreading whatever news was about to come. She was clearly drained at this point and was ready for it to be over.

Dr. Peterson acknowledged their response with a simple head nod. "Well, I've had the pleasure of speaking with him. Firstly, I'd like to say that your son is extremely charming. Usually, when I do these evaluations, people generally aren't as quick to open up and talk with me like he was, so that was a breath of fresh air. He's explained to me that he's just been a little upset lately and that you guys got a bit worried, but other than that he's unaware of why he's here."

Mom let out a mocking laugh, throwing her arms up and crossing them over her chest. Dad shot her a look to let the doctor finish. Dr. Peterson looked down at the clipboard and scribbled something down, almost as if he were evaluating Mom and Dad instead.

"I'm not sure if you're aware of this, but Dillon did write some explicit answers on his intake charts that I questioned him on, and he had a chuckle and claimed that he was just being stupid because of this overreaction from his family," he continued.

Mom and Dad both had the same expression of shock on their faces. Neither of them spoke; their eyes just broadened.

"I did, however, press him more on that subject since you know, those type of answers aren't something that we commonly see here," Dr. Peterson continued. "But after speaking with him, which he's very well spoken by the way, I believe he just didn't channel what he was feeling correctly and was trying to be, well, a smart ass to put it bluntly. Because he does realize that wasn't a rational response and does take ownership for that."

"Wh—what?" Mom uttered, not believing what she was hearing.

"So what do you suggest?" Dad questioned, quickly cutting Mom off.

"Well, like I said, I believe Dillon was being a smart ass and just reacted to get a reaction from you all. He's very calm right now, alert, thinking clearly. I don't see a reason to keep him any longer and would like to start discharge for him. I just wanted to speak with the both of you first to get a stronger feeling for why he was brought here and for any input."

"Well . . . did he tell you about the drugs? Did he tell you about everything he's stolen from me? What about the death threats and disgusting comments he's been making? Did he tell you about his felon of a boyfriend and why they've been trying to get out of the country? Or what about—"

"Rita," Dad butted in once more to stop Mom from getting all worked up again. Dad took the lead and explained everything that's happened thus far and why they have been so concerned for him. Dr. Peterson looked just as confused as they looked after hearing him say that Dillon was clear to go.

"Do you have any of those messages that he sent?" he asked, while looking back down at his clipboard and jotting something down onto the paperwork.

"Yes, I do," Mom answered. She immediately took her phone from her pocket to pull up the text messages between her and Dillon and scrolled up to where the threats started like this was the moment that she's been waiting for. "Just keep scrolling down, there's hundreds for you," she quickly voiced as she leaned forward to hand the doctor her phone.

Dr. Peterson spent a few minutes scrolling down the messages in deep thought; every now and then his eyebrows would dive down in confusion followed by his eyes spreading open and eyebrows rising. Mom and Dad sat there impatiently waiting for feedback. With a deep sigh, Dr. Peterson looked up from the phone and towards Mom and Dad. "Would you mind if I showed these to my team and gave them more of the backstory that you two just explained?" he asked.

"Of course," Mom answered, with cynical hope flowing back through her veins. Dr. Peterson escorted them back to the waiting room while he went to speak with the other members of the psychiatric floor.

"What did they say?" asked Kathy. Mom and Dad weren't even two feet back into the room yet; Dad shook his head in annoyance as he walked closely behind Mom.

"He's charming! He's well-spoken! They're letting him go!" Mom sarcastically shouted.

They're letting him go?! Did I really just hear that?! He did it. He actually did it. He did exactly what he said he was going to do. He played them. He fooled them. Educated professionals fell into his game. They took his bait. Now what? Now what happens? He comes back home with us? We live in fear? He keeps threatening us? He gets away with EVERYTHING he's done once again? Is there no end to this nonsense? What the fuck do we do now? That's it. That's it,

My train of thought was interrupted by the creek of the door opening. Dr. Peterson walked in and took a quick look in the direction of me and Kathy before walking towards Mom on the opposite side of the room and extending out his hand with her cellphone for her to take. Dad stood up to be eye level with him. Mom remained seated, looking up, waiting for some kind of answer. "Well . . . after those messages and the concerns that the two of you have brought to my attention, my team and I think it's best to keep him for a few days. He clearly knows better than to act up here. This isn't a place that one wants to be."

There was a sigh of relief among all of us in that room in that very moment. Mom put her hands up to her face in a praying motion while mouthing, "Thank you, thank you." Dad just nodded his head, glancing over towards Kathy who nodded back before looking at me and sharing a slight we-did-it smile.

"So doc, I do have a question for you. Dillon voluntarily checked himself into this. Now, do you have the power to make him stay? I can't see him agreeing to being held," Dad asked while we all attentively leaned in for the answer.

Wait, that's right. He walked into this willingly. What if he says he's not staying? Can they make him stay? Or can he just get up and walk right out of here?

Dr. Peterson gave a faint smile of support before answering. "No. You see, when someone comes in for a psychological evaluation, even if by their own doing, once they're taken back they give up their rights of walking out. It then becomes solely based on our judgement whether or not we find it suitable and or safe for them to leave. So, he can refuse this all he wants; he's not going anywhere."

There was a minor pause as Dr. Peterson let us appreciate that response. It took a huge weight off of my shoulders, as I'm sure it did the same for Mom and Dad. He continued. "With that being said, I did actually speak with him briefly on this. I told him we were going to keep him a few days and I touched upon the messages that he had sent to you which he sort of had a "realization" moment, so to speak. He didn't say much after that. He kept his stare forward towards the wall."

"So what happens now?" Mom's voice cracked as she struggled to hold herself together. Her heart was breaking. And for a minute I felt her pain. I let myself feel. Although he wasn't my son, he was my brother. My best friend at one point in time. The person I'd laugh for hours with on the floor, dry heaving from prank-calling Dad. The person I'd giggle with as we would take turns running past Mom in the middle of the night when we were supposed to be asleep. She'd be chatting with her friends online while wearing those thick headphones which made it difficult for her to hear what was going on behind her. We would keep going back and forth; it became a game of who would get caught first. He was the person who defended me and looked out for me. The person who once saw a girl on his school bus with my baby doll that I had left behind in the grocery store wagon two days prior. When I couldn't find her and realized that I had lost her, I became hysterical. Turns out the girl on his bus had found her in the wagon and kept her as her own. Dillon went right up to her and said: "That's my sister's doll" and took it. He even placed her on my pillow in my room and when I came home from school that day, there she was. I still have that doll to this day. It's in a box now in the basement along with some of my other toys that I've saved in hopes of showing my kids someday. I probably kept it just because of how much his doing that meant to me, but none the less, I kept it. Now there he was needing me, and I couldn't do anything about it but to lay my trust onto these doctors that they would help him. That's all I wanted. That's all any of us wanted, but I could tell Mom didn't have much faith in that. Understandable, considering they were just about to let him loose.

"From here we're going to admit him; he'll get a room for the night and then sometime tomorrow or the next day, we'll move him to Green's Psychiatric Center depending on when a bed becomes available. It's much nicer there, better equipped. He'll have activities to engage in, be able to speak to peers, see other psychologists; hopefully, he will open up more and be able to get to the bottom of this," Dr. Peterson answered, locking eyes with Mom, placing his hand into the pocket of his scrub coat.

"So he's scared, you think?" Kathy cluelessly asked, inching forward in her seat like she was a little kid leaning in closer to the table, excited as she waited for dessert. I know she didn't intend for it to come across in that way; she wasn't happy over this and she meant it innocently but it's just the way she is.

"Kath. C'mon," Dad responded, shaking his head in irritation, rolling his eyes. I'm not sure why he was always so dismissive of her, or everyone in general for that matter, but this wasn't the time to pick that fight. We were all exhausted, grumpy, and just wanted to get this over with. We'd been here the majority of the day, going on seven hours at this point, and all I could focus on was the grumbling in my stomach.

"Well, he's definitely a bit nervous and like I said earlier, he knows better than to lash out here. This isn't a place someone really wants to be," Dr. Peterson repeated. Mom and Dad thanked him again as he walked out the door.

The four of us sort of just took a minute to look at each other, taking in everything that had happened, letting our emotions have a chance to settle and come down. It began to rain almost on cue. The droplets patted down onto the glass of the window and dribbled down. It was time to go.

"C'mon," Dad spoke from exhaustion, motioning his head towards the door. We followed his lead down the same narrow hall as earlier. The florescent lights beaming down, and the silence of the hall sent a chill down my spine. Once approaching the parking lot, Dad assisted Mom back into the car and handed me the keys to her Explorer which he drove earlier. "Let me know when you get home," he said as he leaned in for a hug and gave me a kiss on the cheek. He held the door open for me as I got into the driver's seat. "Love you, honey," he added in.

"Love you too," I responded back before he closed the door and made his way over to Kathy's car that was parked beside us.

Mom dozed off fairly quickly in the passenger seat on the way home. Her head bobbled down, mouth hung open, and gurgling snores crept in. She was exhausted, for lack of a better word—or shattered. That's more like it. I wish she were awake though; my eyes were beginning to weigh from my own tiredness and the rain fall causing glares in the road from reflections of traffic lights and other cars certainly didn't help. I gently turned the volume of the radio up in an attempt to keep me awake and focused, but Mom seemed to wake briefly, lifting her head, and giving my arm that rested on the center console two comforting pats before drifting back off to sleep. I carefully lowered the volume back down as to not wake her. I wanted her to sleep.

CHAPTER 22:
BLOOD

Mom seemed to be in a somewhat better mood by morning. By the time that I woke up, she was already downstairs in the kitchen drinking a cup of coffee and eating a piece of crumb cake. "Good morning, baby," she muttered through her chewing as I entered the kitchen and bent down for a kiss on the cheek.

"Morning," I replied, taking a seat next to her and stealing a bite of the crumb cake.

"Your father's coming over. He should be here shortly," she informed me, taking a sip of her coffee.

I didn't speak, just nodded my head in confirmation. I guess he was coming to discuss things more in depth. Unless he had an update or something, which I doubt was the case considering it wasn't even noon yet and we all know how delayed places like hospitals are. There's a good chance Dillon was still in the same holding room as last night and hadn't spoken to anyone other than Dr. Peterson yet. But I didn't really care much as to why he was coming. I just wanted to start getting things back together.

Dad and Kathy eventually arrived; they sat at the table on the porch with Mom. Mom had made more coffee and Dad had brought over fresh bagels from the shop. The conversation was light; everyone overall seemed to be in much better spirits. I'm guessing we all finally had a much-needed night of sleep, and it was finally relaxing to have everyone together enjoying breakfast on a warm summer morning thinking the worst was behind us. Kathy eventually brought up the missing items, asking Mom what she planned to do about them. Mom just shook her head, exhaled, and said, "What *can* I do? If they sold them, they're gone. I'm not sure where to even begin with that."

"Hang on," I butted in. "I'm going to go check the car to see if anything they took is in there. You never know." I walked back into the house and grabbed the keys to the car off of the table in the foyer where Dad had placed them yesterday when he drove the car back.

"Good luck," Mom sarcastically spoke as I walked back out past her and down the stairs towards the car. "Whatever you find, you can keep half," she continued as she laughed.

"Yeah, right. Don't tease me," I jokingly responded back. It was nice to hear Mom's humor revive. Even if it was just for a split second.

As I approached the car, I knew nothing of value was going to be left in it. But I kept hoping. I really wanted a little bit of positivity to shine through. I pressed the unlock button on thc kcy fob twice and opened the passenger side door. The scent of fresh linen overwhelmingly flooded my senses as it escaped from the car. I looked around and noticed a full box of dryer sheets torn open and shoved into the pocket on the bottom of the door. *That's weird,* I thought, but proceeded to scan the front driver's side, and passenger-side seats and floors before opening the glove box to see if anything was stashed inside. Slightly disappointed, but highly expected, there was nothing. Only empty cigarette boxes, pens, napkins, and insurance information stored within. I then opened the center console but just found a phone charger and another box of dryer sheets that were ripped open.

I'm not sure why I went to the trunk next instead of the back seat, but for some reason that's exactly what I did. I walked around to the back of the Escape and popped open the trunk. As it lifted, I noticed that the back seats were down and folded over with a towel covering the entirety of the trunk's floor with a bottle of bleach sitting on top of it. And like the front, the trunk also had a box of open dryer sheets stashed into the mesh pocket located on the side of the wall for small storage. That's when my heart began to sink. I don't remember precisely what I was thinking but I just knew this wasn't going to end well. "How's it going over there, detective?" Mom called out in a playful manner. I felt their eyes staring at me from the porch, but I didn't answer. It felt as if I were standing there for ages, though it was really only a few seconds. I stepped forward and slowly peeled the corner of the beige towel back to find a lightened discoloration of the trunk carpet, similar to a bleach stain. I pulled the towel back until it met the bottle of bleach, which was about the half way length of the towel, but didn't proceed because my gut told me not to touch it. The entire area which I had revealed was the same discolored stain, in which I then dropped the towel and took two steps away from the trunk. I never did peek under the rest of the towel, but it was apparent that the bleached area would continue for the full length of it.

With my heart hammering, I hurried back over to the passenger side of the car, rocks shuffling under my feet, and opened the back seat door, staring at the seats folded over. Once again there was a box of open dryer sheets stashed into the pockets of both back doors. I took a deep breath, pulled up the plastic lever located on the side of the back seat and lifted the back rests of the seats up into a straighten position. I let out a gasp and froze in place. "Baby, what's wrong?" Mom called out. I didn't answer. "Riley? Pete, she's turning pale," Kathy said.

Dad hurried down the porch to the car where I was standing. He placed his hands on the back of my shoulders as he looked into the car from behind me. Angered tears began to trickle down my cheek. My breathing was reduced to spotted wheezes each time my heart jumped. "Son of a bitch," Dad muttered as he pushed me to the side, out of view of the back seat. But it was too late. Just like when I was a kid with Shane. I had already seen it.

"Pete?" Kathy questioned.

"What's going on?" Mom worriedly asked.

Dad placed his hands on top of his head and looked over towards Mom and Kathy who were still sitting at the table on the porch and shook his head. I stayed stuck in place, completely numb before anger took over and I began screaming at Dad. "You said you checked the car! You fucking said you checked the car! You said it was fine!"

"Honey. Honey, relax. You have to calm down," he answered while walking towards me with his arms open for an embrace.

"No! Get off me! How did you miss that?! You said you checked it! You said you checked it!" I pushed him off of me and continued to back up. Tears drowning my face as my bones began to shake from rage.

"Riley. Honey. I did check. I took a quick glance. It was late, I thought Dillon was dicking around," he helplessly pled.

"You didn't! You didn't!"

Kathy walked down from the porch, extended her arm around my back, grabbing my opposite shoulder and pulling me into her for a hug. She then carefully led me back towards the porch to Mom, who was still confused as to what exactly was going on, but she opened her arms as I was led up the stairs and then held me. Mom and Kathy directed their look towards Dad, waiting for some kind of answer from him of what the issue was. "What?" mouthed Kathy, attempting to be secretive to shield me from the answer, as if I wasn't the one who just discovered it and knows exactly what's embedded in the cloth of the seats.

"Blood," he mouthed back.

Mom's grip tightened around me. That was her way of saying that it was going to be okay. That she was sorry. That she loved me. That she was here for me. It's astonishing how one simple hug can speak so much. I'm not sure how she does it, but I guess that's what people mean when they talk about a mother's touch. It was instant comfort. My breathing began to slow, and warmth filled my chest. I stood up, breaking Mom's grip as she looked up at me with troubled eyes. The look was reciprocated along with a fake smirk as I turned to open the door to go inside. I needed to take a minute for myself to settle down so I headed for the bathroom to splash some warm water onto my face. Mom and Kathy's eyes followed me through the door, staying silent until it closed behind.

Dad weakly closed the door to the car and slugged his way back up to the porch. "Blood?" Mom questioned. Dad paced back and forth with both of his hands interlocked, resting on the top of his head. He was looking up towards the sky as if he was searching for some kind of answer on what to do or as if he were praying for this not to be reality.

"A lot?" Kathy asked. Dad stopped pacing but didn't respond. He subtly shook his head, exhaled, and just stared at her.

"Pete. The police?" Mom dreadfully probed. It was evident she knew what the answer would be. She had already begun reaching into the pocket of her sweatpants for her phone. I think she just wanted her gut to be wrong.

Dad nodded while letting out a sigh along with a "Yeah" before looking away. He walked towards the edge of the porch, grabbed the railing with both hands, about twelve inches apart from one another, stiffened his grip, and began to shake it a few times out of hopelessness. "Aghhhh!" he yelled out. Kathy excused herself from Mom and made her way over to Dad, placing an open hand on the center of his back, gently rubbing. Mom began to dial 9-1-1.

I stood over the bathroom sink, placing my shaking palms flat onto the granite counter top to support my weight and looked up into the mirror that over hung. I let out a long but silent breath while keeping eye contact with myself in the reflection. The person staring back was at their end. There was nothing left inside of them. Emotionless. Exhausted. Broken.

Fuck. What was that? Was that actually blood? What if he—no. Stop fucking thinking like that! The dark chunks. The splatter. The bleach. The smell. What the fuck is going on?! Is this really happening? What did they do? What did he do? What did he do? What did he do? What the fuck did he do?!

There was a gentle knock on the bathroom door. "Riley, are you okay?" Kathy lightly asked. I remained standing over the sink locked into the mirror, unable to utter words. "Riley?" she asked again.

"Ye—yeah. I'm fine," I managed to answer.

"Are you sure?" she questioned once more.

I shook my stare from the mirror, looking down towards the sink. "Yeah, I'm good," I replied slightly more convincingly than before.

"All right. Well . . . the officers just pulled in. Do you want to come outside?"

I know she meant well, but God, I just wanted to be left alone. "No, I don't," I answered, keeping my head down towards the sink with my eyes scrunched closed, trying to keep myself together.

I stood there for a few more minutes to make sure Kathy had left and was back out front before unlocking the bathroom door. I turned on the warm water from the sink, cupped my hands under the faucet and slowly brought the water up to my face to refresh myself and headed back towards the front door. Instead of going out onto the porch, I quietly stood next to the window to the right of the door that looked out towards the porch so that I could hear what was going on without directly being involved in it. I didn't want to talk to any more police officers, or re-tell the story that seems to never have an ending. But at the same time, I wanted to know what was happening.

By the time I had made it out from the bathroom and to the window, the police officer was just making her way back to the porch from the Escape with Dad. I'm guessing he led her over there and explained what was going on.

"Dillon is your son, correct, ma'am?" the officer questioned, directed at Mom.

"Yes, and Peter is his father," she responded back.

"Okay. And I saw that we were called here not too long ago regarding your son and some threats and a stolen vehicle?"

"Yes, correct."

"And this the vehicle?"

"Yes. It was returned yesterday morning. My ex-husband located where our son was and he drove the car back here yesterday," Mom explained.

"Okay. And where is your son currently?"

"He was admitted into the hospital last night. He went for a voluntary psychological evaluation. He's either still there or being transferred to Green's Psychiatric Center. I haven't received an update as of yet," Mom replied.

"Okay. I'll get more information from you in a minute. I'm going to call my supervisor and sort this out. See where he wants to take this," the officer conveyed as she turned to walk down the steps of the porch with her right hand on her radio which was attached to the uniform on her chest, getting ready to speak into it.

"Wait, officer. What's the take on the car? Is it blood?" Mom eagerly but hesitantly asked before the officer was able to make it down the stairs.

"Yeah. It definitely resembles blood of some sort. I'll discuss further in depth after speaking with my supervisor," she responded in a stern tone and made her way back to her vehicle, paging on her radio with a muffled voice.

About ten minutes later, the door to the patrol car opened and the officer made her way back to the porch.

"Did Dillon give any more information on the car or the stains?" the officer inquired, switching her stare back and forth from Mom to Dad.

"No, just that Damien took the car, returned without it and that he was afraid there would be blood in it," Dad answered.

Mom rolled her eyes at Dad's answer and continued with "He told his father that Damien was trying to get them out of the country and took the car but wouldn't elaborate any further on what he meant by that."

The officer nodded her head while giving a slow blink and exhale as if what she was about to say was going to be something that Mom and Dad didn't want to hear. "All right, yeah. Just wanted to clarify there. So I spoke with my supervisor, sent over the photos, and gave the run down on what was going on and, unfortunately, unless Dillon has more information and comes forward about what happened and what those stains are, there's really not anything that can be done."

Mom, Dad, and Kathy sat there dumbfounded as I let out a slight laugh in disbelief from behind the wall. *He's really going to get away with all of this*, I thought.

"What do you mean there's nothing you can do? There's—there's blood in the car," Mom said.

"I understand your concern. But that could have been caused by a number of things; maybe they hit an animal and put it on the seat to get it out of the road, or maybe it's not even blood. Something could have spilt."

"You said yourself it's blood. I don't understand"

"Listen, I get it. I shouldn't have said that, though in my opinion it does resemble blood. Yet, it could also be a number of other things like I said. The only true way to determine exactly what it is would be to send it out for forensics, but my supervisor and team aren't troubled about it. You know, there's no body, there's no crime scene, there's nothing more to lead us to believe this is something more than what it is. So, unless Dillon comes forward with something else, there's no further action that we can take."

"Right. Fantastic. So I'm just going to sit here with a bloody car parked in my driveway like it's nothing!"

"Rita. Please," Dad spoke softly with a stressful stare.

"Right, right. I'll stop cause what the hell am I supposed to do with it?! Leave it here? Drive it around? Let it fucking ferment?"

"C'mon, Rita," Dad tried to chime in.

"No, no. Really. Officer, what am I supposed to do with it? Tell me. Do I take it to the car wash? Let them call the police on *me* for bringing in a fucking blood-stained car? Do I sit here and play in it? Seriously. Tell me what I'm supposed to fucking do," Mom continued to spiral scenarios off of her tongue.

"I understand, ma'am. You're free to do what you'd like with the vehicle. I can go ahead and give you a copy of the report made today and if you have further issues down the line, you can give us a call back."

"Wow. You stand here and say it resembles blood and after knowing everything we have told you and the mental state my son has been in and tells his father that he's afraid of there being blood in the car, you stand here and tell me there's nothing that can be done? No samples taken? No further analysis? Just throw your hands up and walk away? Damien was on the most wanted list! Who the hell knows what this man is capable of!" Mom angrily argued.

"Like I said ma'am, I can give you a copy of the report made today and—"

"Yeah. Go and do that," Mom interrupted, turning her head away from the officer, biting her lip and slamming a fist onto the table.

That's it? That's the end of it? Is that really what just happened? How is there nothing further that can be done?! What does she mean there's no crime scene?! What do they call that then? There's blood splattered, smeared into the seats! There's bleach stains in the trunk! There's chunks of gooey matter shriveled up and dried in the blackened crimson! And what about the overwhelming smell of linen trying to mask the odor of the car?! How much closer to text book crime can a person get? No further testing? Really? Not even taking a sample of it to see if anything pops up in the data base or in case something comes up later on? Wow. This must be why there's so many open and unsolved cases out there. For shitty handling like this! What now? We just move on from this? Go on about our days like none of this ever happened? And he just gets away? He just gets away with it?

CHAPTER 23:
DIVERTED BLAME

I couldn't get my body to pause that night. Twisting and turning in bed. My mind wouldn't shut off. The panic in my chest wouldn't settle. But what else was new? The possibility that Dillon could have killed someone replayed in my head every time I closed my eyes. The countless scenarios: my thoughts spiraled out of control. Then came the guilt of even suspecting he'd be capable of something as horrific as this. *What kind of sister am I? What kind of person thinks this sort of thing of their brother without giving them the benefit of doubt first?*

The only time that I could recall feeling genuinely scared for my life with him is back when I was maybe six or seven years old, and that doesn't really count. We were playing explorers in the back yard when a racoon came darting out of the bushes towards us and we took off running. I was ahead of him, only by a few steps, he grabbed the back of my Rugrats t-shirt and yanked me behind him, right into the racoon. But even then I think I was more upset over my favorite shirt being stretched out than me thinking Dillon tried to kill me. We've even grown to laugh about it through the years. Don't get me wrong. I was petrified in the moment, and I thought I *was* going to die, but that's the only experience I have to support this, and I can't count something like that as "evidence." I was seven; we were kids. If I were to walk into the police station today to report that as attempted murder, I would be laughed at. It's silly. I mean, even with Shane. I've always felt something off about that situation, but I've never sat down to dissect it or actually question if Dillon had anything to do with that until all of this started. It never crossed my mind. I felt safe with him. And now? Now I can't get the nauseating thoughts out of my head!

"Did he sound okay?" Mom's voice traveled down the hall into my room.

"All right . . . let me know how it goes . . . yeah, I'll talk to you later . . . yeah, bye," she continued.

"Riley, baby, can you come in here for a minute?" Mom called out from her room.

"Yeah, one sec," I mumbled as I dreadfully rolled out of bed and slogged my way to the door.

"I just spoke with your father; he talked to Dillon. He's in Green's, got moved there yesterday morning like we thought," Mom explained as I sat down next to her on her bed.

"He spoke to him? Why did they tell you he wasn't there for phone calls when you tried calling last night?" I asked.

"Yeah, turns out he's just not taking phone calls from me. Told your father this is all my fault. Claims that he's only there because of how I want to control him, how manipulative I am, and that I'm looking for attention."

"Of course it's your fault in his eyes. He doesn't see responsibility or accountability for anything—nothing is him. Mom, he truly believes that."

Mom didn't answer; she looked at me then looked down at the floor, wiping a tear from her eye.

"Did he say anything else? Did he ask him about the blood?" I knew I shouldn't have asked that, but it was like word vomit, and I couldn't hold it back. It was the only thing rerunning in my mind and the only thing I cared about in that moment. Mom slowly turned her face back towards me with furrowed eyebrows and a locked stare. "No, Riley, he didn't. You can't just ask something like that over the phone when the line is being recorded," she snipped sternly.

"Okay, all right, I'm sorry," I apologized as I got up from her bed and made my way back towards her door. Mom plainly wasn't in the mood, and I didn't want to end up in an argument with her. I just wanted to be alone at this point and I'm sure she did as well. "He's going to visit him later today. I'll let you know when I hear back," Mom

muttered softly. I nodded in acknowledgement and closed
the door behind me.

CHAPTER 24:
VISITATION: PART 1

Dad pulled up to Green's Psychiatric Hospital and it looked like a vacation resort. I've always imagined psych hospitals to be dark brick buildings that tower toward the sky. I pictured them hidden away in secluded areas lurking behind tall trees, glooming underneath the moon with wired fencing and bar-lined windows. But I guess that's just a look for the movies. Green's had beautiful landscaping with large glass windows filling the rooms with light. There were different buildings for different uses: dorms, a recreation center, a library, and a hopeful water fountain in the center. Kind of like a college campus.

Dad backed into a spot facing the main entrance, but didn't get out. He watched attentively as people entered and exited through the sliding glass doors and anxiously tapped the steering wheel with his fingers. I'm sure he was contemplating what the next move was, what he would say to Dillon, what Dillon would say to him, what kind of mood Dillon would be in, what side of Dillon he would get, the answers he would receive, and if he truly even wanted to hear the answers. Sometimes it's better not knowing. It's easier that way. To create your own narrative. One that makes it easier to live with. Dad lit a cigarette, turned off the ignition and paced his way towards the front doors.

"Welcome to Green's; is there something I can help you with, sir?" a friendly voice projected from behind the check-in counter.

"Yeah, hi, how are you? I'm here for um, Dillon Venturi," Dad nervously replied as he placed his keys onto the counter and reached into his back pocket to get his ID.

"Of course, let me just check you in and we'll have Dillon down in a few moments."

"And sir, one last question, do you have any weapons, drugs, cigarettes, sharp objects, or any metal on you?"

"Ah, uh no. No, just my wallet and keys," Dad responded while quickly patting his pockets to make sure that he left his lighter in the car.

"Okay, thank you. You can walk down this hall to your right to the family lounge and Dillon will meet you there. Here's your license back sir, but I do need you to leave your keys here. It's a safety protocol."

"Of course. No problem, thank you." Dad placed his ID into his leather wallet, stuck it back into the back pocket of his jeans and made his way towards the hall.

Dad took a seat at one of the café-style tables set to the left in the room to wait for Dillon. The room had a handful of families visiting their loved ones. Some laid out on the couches watching TV that hung on the wall as if they were at home in their own living room while others sat at tables playing card games, laughing, and smiling. Then there was Dad—off to the side, tapping his foot, staring at the door waiting for Dillon to walk through. He began to worry that Dillon had changed his mind about the visit and was refusing to come as he had been waiting there for nearing twenty minutes when the door finally squeaked open, and Dillon walked in. Dad stood up and gave him a one-armed hug. Dillon nodded and sat down across from him. He was wearing a white pajama-like sweat suit and slippers.

"You look good bud." Dad broke the ice.

Dillon nodded. "Yeah, I love it here." He smirked.

"You love it here? Really, Dillon?"

"What? Yeah, I do. I've made a lot of friends, the fridges are stocked, and I can eat and drink whatever I want whenever I want and all for free!"

Dad shook his head in disappointment, "Really? You can't take something serious for two freakin minutes, can you? Everything is a joke to you."

Dillon painted a patronizing smile across his face, "Don't. Don't come here and start yelling at me because this isn't turning out how you guys wanted it to. Okay?

This was supposed to be a punishment? You can go and tell Rita she's going to have to try harder for that big guy."

"Big guy? Ha, okay. All right. No one's here to punish you, Dillon. This wasn't a game. This wasn't some big scheme made up by your mother for her enjoyment like you seem to think it is. And all of this? All of this is making her sick, Dillon. It's not helping."

"Yes. Oh, yes, Daddy. I made her sick. I made her sick. I'm the reason she's a crippled bitch too, right?" Dillon interrupted with laughter in his tone.

"That's your mother you're talking about," Dad firmly whispered while placing his fist onto the table. Dillon was getting to him. He knew exactly how to tick him off. Two things that he hated the most was when one of us would laugh in his face while being scolded, or speaking poorly of Mom, which Dillon was presently doing both. Dillon knew Dad couldn't cause a scene in the middle of the facility or do anything to him for that matter. He was having a field day pissing him off.

"You know what, buddy? Forget it. That's not why I'm here"

"Ah, let me guess, Mommy wants an autograph from her son in the insane asylum, huh?" Dillon grinned.

"Damnit, Dillon. Just listen to me for a damn second," Dad uttered through his teeth, looking straight into Dillon's eyes. "There was blood found in your car."

Immediately, Dillon's demeanor changed. The smirk was washed from his face, his eyes became smaller, and his body tensed.

"What blood?"

"What blood? I don't know, Dillon; you tell me."

"I don't know what you're talking about."

Dad looked around briefly in disbelief. "You told me when we were picking up the car that you were afraid there was going to be blood in it."

"No, I didn't," Dillon spit out before Dad even finished his sentence.

Dad was speechless. He gave a puzzled stare as if there were a possibility that he made this all up in his head. For a moment, Dad almost believed him. Dillon was good at that. He was great at making you feel like what happened never happened and making you feel like *you're* the one becoming delusional. It's a shame, really, that he never followed through with his acting pursuit. He would have been a star; I can tell you that.

Our parents took Dillon to pageant after pageant starting when he was around three or four years old. He was always taking center stage at family parties and gatherings— singing, dancing, telling stories and making people laugh. Oh, and don't get me started on the countless hours of him forcing us to sit on the couch as he would play different movies and films on the TV while he acted the entire thing out. Every scene. Every character. Every song. Every word. If you don't believe me, I can pull out the family videos— there must be over a dozen of them. By the time he reached middle school, he was getting leads in the drama productions and choir concerts; he lit up on stage. He looked like that's where he belonged and others saw it too, so it wasn't any surprise when he started to show serious interest in acting by the end of middle school. Mom and Dad, of course, jumped on this and took Dillon around to shop for agents until they found one. From there came the photo shoots and head shots, to finally an audition. It seemed as if things were coming together for him, until, well . . . it wasn't.

Mom and Dad decided to take a trip out to New York City with Dillon for a modeling audition. His agent seemed confident that this would do wonders and open doors of opportunity for him and without any doubts the trip was booked. Although I stayed behind with our grandparents, I was excited for him. I mean, at that age I thought my brother was going to be famous and that it was going to be the coolest thing ever. He seemed excited about it too, but then something changed. When they got back, Dillon didn't speak much about it. He held himself as if he never even went in the first place. Later on, Mom told me that he never made it to his actual audition. She said while they were in the waiting room Dillon was flipping through the pages of his photo portfolio when all of a sudden, he closed the book and said he wanted to go. He stood up and walked out. Mom and Dad tried talking with him, tried understanding what happened but Dillon just insisted that he didn't want to do it anymore. "I'm over it" was his exact wording.

Still, to this day, none of us are really sure what the reasoning was or what happened. It was like a switch went off and he just dropped it. I think maybe he didn't like the photos of himself. Maybe his self-esteem got to him, or the bullying. We're not sure. All I can say is that the transition into his first year of high school was rough. He started high school two weeks after his New York trip and it wasn't long before the fall choir concert, which ended up being his last. Mid performance, Dillon began unbuttoning his white-collared shirt that everyone had to wear to expose a baby blue one underneath. Dillon was center in the back row; there were four rows, each row raised slightly higher than the one in front so that when the students took their places on stage, everyone could be seen. It wasn't long after that that Dillon began crouching behind the person in front of him and popping up sporadically with a look of surprise on his face. Then came the "claw grabs." While crouched down behind the kid in front of him, Dillon's hand would then raise up behind the kid's shoulders in a crab-claw grabbing manner and begin to grab at the kid's hair and ears. The kid tried keeping his focus and tried to ignore the nuisance that was happening, but that only seemed to egg Dillon on further as he would pop his head up like before, but only now he would let out screams that cracked with laughter. It looked as if he was a little kid playing hide and seek. I couldn't help but laugh. Mom even broke out in hysterics. Dad, on the other hand, seemed quite embarrassed and shrunk into his seat. It made sense now why Dillon begged us to sit in the front row of the auditorium. The audience, however, had mixed responses as well. Some burst out in giggles and smiles, while others had looks of disgust and anger.

Eventually the choir director yanked Dillon off stage during one of the transitions and a few minutes later approached us at our seats while the concert was in intermission. "Are you Dillon's parents?" he asked sternly. I was seated between Mom and Dad. Dad was seated at the end seat and shook his head "No" while crossing his arms, refusing to even look in the way of the director. Mom let out a huff and shot a nasty look at Dad as she got up. "I'm his mother," she spoke and followed the director out of the auditorium, discreetly punching Dad in the arm as she passed over. I stayed seated with Dad. Some parents were smiling and laughing at her, telling her they had it all on tape. Others grabbed her arm as she was walking by and said things like "Your son ruined this entire night." Mom just bit her lip to stop her from smiling and continued out the door. Dillon was booted from the choir after that and given a two-day after-school detention sentence.

Later on in the year was the school's drama production of *The Phantom of the Opera*, when Dillon pulled a similar stunt. He pranced onto stage when it wasn't his scene and danced around in the back—skipping, spinning, and giggling with his mic on. The curtains finally closed for "technical difficulties" and Dillon was pulled off once again. Like the choir incident, the drama teacher approached us at our seats and escorted me and Mom to the office. Dad refused to even show up that night; he was still horribly embarrassed from the last event, so I guess that was the right call. Like choir, Dillon was obviously kicked from drama, but it didn't seem to bother him in the slightest.

At that moment in time, I thought it was funny; so did Mom. I'm sure Dad did as well but was just too embarrassed to be confronted with it in front of an audience; nonetheless, looking back on it now, it was a pivotal moment. Everything Dillon ever wanted, he walked away from. The modeling, the singing, the acting—he just threw away with no care in sight. And that's when his antics in school really jump-started full force. Maybe this crisis was overlooked because this change in him happened during a transitional period from middle school into high school, making it easy for everyone to pass it off as being adolescent behavior—typical rebellion, as opposed to it signaling some type of psychological or mental emergency.

I wonder how things would have played out if this "break" had happened later on in his life. Would it have been more of a red flag? Would someone have noticed something wasn't right? That something was brewing in the shadows of his mind? I remember learning in college that a vast majority of psychological disorders begin revealing symptoms by age fourteen, though often go unnoticed for several years, not leading to a diagnosis until as late as twenty-four or twenty-five years old. This has literally all been right on point, statistically. It's all making sense now. Why aren't teachers, counselors, etc. trained more in this area? How many kids slip through the system and are punished and labeled a "trouble maker" when in actuality there's mental switches being turned on? Catching disorders early is key to better outcomes in life with learning how to manage them and work through them. If only someone would have noticed this sooner, they could have helped him. We all could have helped him. Just the fact that he dropped everything that ever meant anything to him within an instant should have grabbed someone's attention. The stage is what he loved since a toddler. How was that not enough to grab the eyes of all who knew him? It wasn't like he was coming home late, or out drinking with his friends. That I would call typical behavior from a teenager. But this? This was a life-altering decision made seemingly in the blink of an eye. How wasn't that noticed?

CHAPTER 26:
VISITATION: PART 2

"Dillon . . . you looked me in the eye while finding your car and told me you were afraid there would be blood in it. You told me that Damien was trying to get you out of the country," Dad firmly whispered while leaning in towards Dillon, cautious for others not to hear.

Dillon looked helpless for a moment. As if there were nowhere to turn. Like life just became real. He was panicking. I'm sure Dad thought he would crack, but nope. "I was just joking," he muttered with a faint laugh.

Dad made eye contact and clenched his teeth. "No. You weren't kidding. That wasn't a joke. You said it, you were fearful, and now there's blood."

"Well, I don't know how it got there," Dillon responded with a straight face. It was almost like he was mocking the situation. Dad had enough of it. He realized Dillon wouldn't break and that he would get nowhere with the conversation. Dad wanted to yell. He wanted to cause a scene. He wanted to take a hold of Dillon and throw him up against the wall. To look him in the eyes. To make him understand the severity of the circumstances. To get through to him. To get him to knock his shit off. But he couldn't. Not there. Dillon knew that. He knew that he was safe right where he was— that Dad couldn't do a single thing to him. That he could be as big of a smart-ass as he wanted to be, and that Dad had to take it.

"Hm. Okay, buddy. Just wanted to make you aware that the police are going to question you on this, and if you lie or cover up or continue to play this fantasyland game, that you're going to go down for this just as much as Damien will. And that will be the end of it." Dad continued to whisper through his teeth.

"At least we'll be together," Dillon snarled back.

Dad was at a loss. He thought for sure that would have scared him. *Was Dillon not afraid of the police or did he just call Dad's bluff? Maybe he was just that full of himself that even when presented with something as serious as this that he felt—or should I say, he knew—he was untouchable?* Dad's eyes grew and fixated deeply on Dillon's. Dad's face became tight, and his fists clenched as he took a deep breath in and held it. Dillon flashed a sarcastic grin and leaned back in the chair. Like he was relaxed. Like he hit a jackpot. Dad stood up, keeping eye contact with Dillon, lightly knocking his fist onto the table two times as a signal that he was giving up, gave a nod of the head, and walked out of the visitation lounge.

Dillon sat there for a few minutes, ostensibly unbothered. Who knows what was going on in his head, but I'm sure he would want us to think that he felt accomplished and like he won. As if there were anything to "win" in a situation like this, though I can only wish he felt some type of fear or worry. Not that I want him to be afraid, but more so that I can know that he's capable of feeling some type of emotion. Some type of empathy. Some type of understanding of the real world and what consequences can be. I can only hope that this appearance of him not caring, and mocking is only an act. I *pray* it's an act. I would rather this be a sick tactic, that maybe he's just afraid of looking weak by showing emotions and letting others in than actually not feeling anything at all. Or finding genuine amusement from the pain of others. If that's the case, if he's unable to feel, if he really finds humor in any of this, who knows what he's truly capable of? And that's what terrifies me.

CHAPTER 27:
ACCESS DENIED

I had a breaking moment. I couldn't sit around any longer waiting to see how things would unfold. I needed answers. I needed something. The amount of anxiety that was infesting my body had taken its toll and became desperate for relief. While Mom was in the bathroom, I quietly paced myself past the door and into her bedroom to grab Dillon's cell phone off of the top of her dresser. I slid it into the pocket of my sweatpants and quietly made my way back past the bathroom door and into my room, well, as quiet as I could be. Hershey decided to follow behind, which I'm sure Mom heard the jingles of his dog tags clanking together on his collar. But on the bright side, it probably drowned out the sounds of my footsteps creaking past. I bet Hershey was judging me, as he didn't fully enter Mom's room with me. He stayed at the door frame, peaking his head in to watch what I was doing, as if he'd get in trouble if he came any further. Dogs have a funny way of knowing when things aren't right, but I'm going to pretend that he was acting as my lookout by helping me blend in the sound of my steps instead.

I didn't feel guilty now as I did when I entered Dillon's room days ago. I didn't feel like I was doing anything wrong this time. I felt eagerness, and a bit of excitement if I'm being honest. I didn't feel like I was invading his privacy. I felt I had a right this time to know, considering all of the fucking hell he's put us through. Now? Now it was time to get to the bottom of this . . . so I thought. As quickly as my excitement filled, it deflated just as fast as I pressed the screen button on his phone to find out he had put a passcode on it. I've seen Dillon use his phone time and time again and never did he ever have it locked. I tried two different eight-digit numbers (yes, he put his passcode on eight digits rather than the usual four-digit code most people use). I tried his birth date with two digits for the month, two for the day and four for the year but was denied. I tried once more using our mother's birth date in the same format and once again was denied. I didn't want to try for the third time, due to security measures that lock the phone completely for a certain amount of time after three failed attempts. If I was going to try for a third, I wanted to make sure I spent time thinking of it first.

Why the lock now? Is there something all of a sudden now worth hiding? When did he do it? When did he think he would be without his phone? Wait—maybe this was all planned. Maybe he locked up his phone on the way to the hospital, knowing he'd be admitted and be without it. Maybe he did it as a precaution so that the doctors at the hospital wouldn't be able to rummage through it when collecting his belongings. Or maybe it goes deeper than that. Maybe his phone wasn't accidentally left on the car. Maybe this was his plan all along as another psychological "fuck you" to us. This could be him taunting us even more, knowing that one of us would take it and attempt to go through it. Knowing that his phone holds all of the information that we want. After all, how did he forget it on the car? The music was blasting from it. Didn't he hear the music slowly fading lower and lower into the distance as he walked further away and into the facility? He had to have heard it! This had to be a set up. He had to know.

I sat a few moments at my desk in defeat. *Just another brick wall,* I thought. Then an idea popped into my head. Maybe his text notifications aren't private as I noticed on his lock screen there were notifications from SocialFriends of comments and messages waiting for him. If his texts aren't private, then I can access his email and even his social media accounts. I can press "forgot password" at login and it will send a temporary code to his phone which I would then have to enter into his email or social media login page to reset the password to the account. There had to be messages or something of value on either

SocialFriends or his email, especially if he had his phone storage linked to the email. Maybe I'm not at a total loss. The only issue was that since the code wouldn't be coming from a smart phone device to a smart phone, but rather from a computer-generated number, the text wouldn't be delivered as his service was disconnected. But I had a way around that one as well.

Mom used to shut off my service often growing up as a punishment, but what she didn't know was that I had access to her account since I was the one who helped her set up her password. All I would have to do was log into her account and enter the code to re-activate my line and just like that I had my service back. The only thing was, I had to make sure to keep my volume off and only use it when Mom wasn't around. She had no idea as I made sure to de-activate it right before she was about to lift the punishment so she wouldn't notice. I'm sure I'll end up telling her all about it years from now when I'm older so she can't get mad over it and hopefully have a laugh. But that's all I had to do here as well: activate, then de-activate; so I grabbed my laptop and powered it on.

With Dillon's service now being activated, I continued on with the rest of my plan. I held my breath as I submitted the email password reset to be sent to the number on file. My heart was pounding. If his text notifications were private, it would just read "new message" and wouldn't show a preview of the text along with it. If they weren't private, a notification would pop up reading the name or number the message was from along with a line or two of the message, hopefully enough to catch a glimpse of the code. This was the moment of truth. If they were private, I was out of options and answers. Then his screen lit up and my worries vanished. There it was. The code. "Your temporary passcode is 4-6-2-7." I got it. That was all I needed. I typed the code into the password box on the login page of his email and was brought to the page to create a new password. Adrenaline returned. I was in. *Got ya*, I thought to myself as a smile swept my face.

The smile didn't last long as what I was met with in Dillon's email was not what I was expecting or looking for. I honestly don't even want to repeat or explain any of it as that's not the way I wanted to ever see my brother but all I will say is that the email was extremely graphic, violent, and concerning, which isn't my story to tell. As quickly as I mistakenly clicked on the email which was labeled "The handbook of Dillon's sexual evolution" was as quickly as I clicked out of it. I was intending to click the email below it as it was to Damien, but my laptop froze and I ended up opening that one instead, which was pinned at the top. Pinning an email means that you make it so that it is kept up top as the very first email to be seen; usually, people will pin ones of importance. After clicking out of that error I actually decided to log out of his email all together as I was greatly disturbed at what I had read, and it was clear that his text messages were not linked to his email. I was solely looking for insight on this current situation, not an autobiography written about himself in the third person expressing how he enjoys to be tased, encourages forced drug use and rape, how he's been on a mission to contract STDs and how him seeking homeless men for sexual pleasure started at the age of fourteen.

I contemplated for over an hour if I should continue to access his SocialFriends page or not. I was too stunned after what I came across in his email but ultimately decided to carry on as I was positive there would be something of value. I took another few moments to try to shake the disturbing thoughts of his email from my memory and made my way to SocialFriends. I reset that password just as easily as I did his email. I instantly went to his messages and scrolled through until I came to Damien's. This time I made sure not to stray into anyone else's message thread except for the ones I was strictly looking for to avoid another email mishap.

There wasn't anything much at first. Regular conversations, things one would expect from two people in a relationship, though they seemed to be mostly one-sided from Dillon with not many responses from Damien. I continued to skim through anyway until I got to the more recent ones. "Have to talk through here, babe. The cunt shut off my line." Damien responded with a thumbs up emoji as Dillon continued with "She's going to fucking pay. Mark my words, baby" followed by seventeen messages that just read "pay," which all had no response. *Even your felon boyfriend thinks you're psychotic*, I thought with a chuckle. Then the messages started to get weird. "Babe, be careful with the car; it really is reported stolen." "I just talked to my Dad. This isn't a joke, babe." As the hours went on, Dillon continuously sent messages to Damien that went unanswered.

Dillon: "Babe, where are you?"
    "Are you okay?"
    "Babe, please. Where are you?"
    "Did you get caught?"
    "Omg"
    "Are you leaving me?"
    "Babe"
    "Don't leave me, babe. Please"
    "Did the cops come?"
    "Tell me what's going on"
    "Are you hurt?"
    "Don't leave me here"
The messages stopped there until the following afternoon when they
    continued:
    "Bring my fucking car back"
    "Bring it back right now"
    "You are a piece of shit"
    "Bring back the fucking car"
    "I can end you"

Once again, the messages went unanswered until around midnight when Dillon sent another message that read, "I love you, baby."

However, this time Damien answered. "Hey, I will be back soon. This is going to sound completely embarrassing but I shit myself and had to pull over. It was a mess."

Dillon responded back with "LOL baby, it happens." Damien continued with "Had to run into the convenience store for new pants and left the car. I am walking back to the apartment".

I'm sorry, what? What the hell was that? What do I even make of any of that? Damien "disappears" with the car and two days later responds with he shit himself? What grown fucking man shits himself, parks the car on the side of the road in the middle of the night, and walks himself over an hour back to his place? And he pays no mind to the craziness that Dillon started to stir? No response to anything Dillon was saying? No reactions? Just "Hey, sorry I shit myself"? I'm not buying that. That's not sitting right with me. That's . . . that's fucking ridiculous.

The next and the last few messages Dillon sent were from after Dad had driven out to pick Dillon up. The first one read, "Babe, I'm sorry. I'm going to come back. I just got freaked out. I need time to clear my head." This went unanswered. The next one seemed to be from the following morning:

"LOL, the health department came to the house."

"My Dad gave me the letter."

"I know this is going to sound crazy but I don't want to get rid of it because you gave it to me."

"I want to keep you with me forever."

"They think I'm a health risk—isn't that funny?"

"I'm going to keep it forever, babe. This was your gift to me and it is not being taken away."

"Ever."

"I will do God's work and share you with others"

"HA"

The last message was dated from when he was going to the hospital after the "intervention" with us. It simply read, "Baby, I won't let them tear us apart. They think I'm crazy but I'm only crazy for you. Please wait for me." I sat there puzzled at the screen, trying to make sense of the mess that I had just read through.

I clicked out of his and Damien's messages and scrolled through to see if there were messages from anyone else who seemed sketchy or odd.

What the hell was that? He needs help. He needs so much fucking help. What the hell is he talking about? What did Damien give to him? Health risk? What? What made him so scared to leave? What did they do? What happened? Why isn't Damien responding to anything? What the hell is Dillon doing?!

My train of thought was interrupted by the sound of a car door closing in the driveway. I scooted the chair back from the desk and went over to peak out of the blinds of my window to see Jennifer walking towards the front door. "Mom, Jen is here," I called out.

"Who?" she asked.

"Jennifer," I repeated as I leaned down over my desk to click out of SocialFriends before making my way down the stairs to greet her.

CHAPTER 28:
BACKTRACKING

"Hey, I'm sorry to just drop by. Are you and Mama busy?" Jennifer asked.

I shook my head. "No, not at all. Mom said she'll be down in a minute." I motioned for her to come in. We took a seat on the couch in the living room as Mom made her way down the stairs.

"Hey sweetie, how are you?" Mom asked as she approached the entrance to the living room.

"Hey, Mama, all is good; how are you doing? I'm sorry for stopping by unannounced," Jen responded back.

Mom assured her that she was always welcome and that she would never be a bother to her as she sat down on the sofa chair next to the couch. "So what pays this visit, sweetheart?" Mom questioned.

"I just wanted to check in on you. See how you were doing and if you needed anything. I know there's a lot going on," Jen answered.

"Oh, you know—just the usual. Dillon's claiming I'm the bad guy in all of this with a master plan of sending him away," Mom sarcastically joked.

"Yeah, I heard." Jennifer chuckled back with an eye roll. "I just finished visiting with him, actually."

Mom's eyes widened. "You did?" she asked. Mom straightened herself up in the chair to listen more attentively to what Jennifer had to say. I was curious as well but stayed slouched on the couch to play it cool.

"I did, yeah," she responded and continued on with how Dillon's living in his fantasy world of how he's done no wrong and how she was trying to get through to him that how he's been acting isn't okay. She told him she was worried about him and called him out on how he's been treating Mom. Jennifer claimed that he started to admit that he had fucked up and that he was just mad and wanted reactions out of people. But that could have just been a ploy for him. He knew who he could pull one over on and who he couldn't. He knew Jennifer always called him out on his bullshit and wouldn't stand for any of it.

"Did he say anything about the murder?" I chimed in. Mom shot me the death stare. The "shut-the-hell-up" look. I knew that would piss her off, but I played innocent.

"The murder?" Jennifer questioned with a confused tone as her mouth hung open, her eyes squinted. She looked at me then back at Mom, waiting for an explanation.

"There's no murder," Mom sighed. "When we went looking through his car, we noticed what looks like blood splattered on the back seat."

"Wait—what?" Jennifer looked even more confused than before.

Mom rolled her eyes as if this was some crazy scenario that I made up in my head, once again trying to lessen the severity of what Dillon was doing. "Listen, I don't know," she answered, shaking her head in a disapproving manner. "Pete said when he had gone to pick Dillon up, that Dillon had mentioned something about being afraid to get the car. He mentioned there being blood or something in it, but we all know Dillon. He plays games and creates stories to get a rise. I wouldn't be surprised if he went down to the party store and picked up a bottle of fake blood to trickle over the seats."

"Okay, so we're making excuses for murder now?" I cut in with a laughter of disbelief. I bit my lip and looked down at my phone in hand, scrolling through the first app that I clicked on to disengage myself from the situation. I couldn't believe she was trying to make it sound like what was happening wasn't actually happening. This entire time she was in agreement that there was blood smeared on the inside of the car. She called the police; it's still sitting in our driveway because she doesn't know where to get a blood-stained car detailed and cleaned! But now she wants to sit here and act like nothing has happened?

Mom retorted, "Damnit, Riley, he didn't even have the car! Damien took it!" I felt her stare lock in on me.

"Yeah, of course he's gonna say that," I muffled.

"Well, I knew about Damien taking the car," Jennifer added. "Dillon actually face-timed me a few nights ago freaking out and upset. He said he didn't know what Damien was doing, that he had taken the car and Dillon wasn't sure what he was capable of. He seemed in a real panic over it."

Mom glanced towards me with a sly smirk, thinking Jennifer's comment somehow validated her belief that Dillon had nothing to do with the car missing. "Yeah, cause that doesn't seem like a planned alibi or anything," I mumbled once again.

"Now he's making up alibis, Riley? The kid had a fucking mental break," Mom angrily snipped back as her facial expression tightened.

"Whatever. I'm done here. Think what you want," I answered as I threw my hands up in a surrendering motion and got up from the couch.

"Guys, c'mon," Jennifer interrupted, trying to make peace. Mom muttered something in response under her breath when I was already at the front door putting on my sneakers. I was just out of reach of hearing what it was that she was saying, but knowing her I knew it was a smart-ass remark that instantaneously shot fuel through my body. I walked back over to the living room entrance, yelling: "ALL YOU DO IS FUCKING DEFEND HIM! HE DOES NO WRONG IN ANYONE'S EYES! YOU LET HIM GET AWAY WITH EVERYTHING! YOU KNOW WHAT? THIS IS ALL YOUR FUCKING FAULT! YOU LET HIM BE LIKE THIS! SO DON'T COME TO ME ANYMORE CRYING AND TELLING ME THAT YOU'RE SCARED OF HIM WHEN YOU'RE JUST GOING TO REPEAT DOING THE SAME FUCKING THINGS!"

Jennifer hurried up from the couch and came over to me to try to get me to calm down. She tried grabbing my arms, but I pushed her away and started storming off towards the door to leave.

"And while you're at it, why don't you ask him about Damien shitting himself and leaving the car on the side of the road, then walking home! Because that story sounds legitimate for a forty-something year old to do, right?!" I screamed while grabbing my keys off the wall hook and slammed the door shut as I heard Mom asking what the hell I was talking about.

Tears of frustration ran from my face as I made my way over to my car. I sat in the driveway for a few minutes with my head resting on the steering wheel trying to calm myself down before heading off. I had no idea where I was going but I needed to get away from the situation. Everything was becoming too much to handle, and Mom wasn't making anything better. She always does this though. I'm not sure why I was surprised or expected something different from her this time around. She always talks a big game. She acts one way in front of me than completely switches up her thoughts with someone else. I truly thought this time got through to her, but its apparent she's going to start backing down and reverting to what's easiest for her—to act like nothing is happening.

I ended up parking down by the bay to sit with my thoughts as I watched and listened to the waves clashing onto shore. I felt so alone. It was like everyone formed a team against me. Like I was the bad guy in this. Like I was in the wrong. Everyone seemed to think that I was the crazy one, jumping to conclusions and making mountains out of ant hills. But maybe I am the issue here. I've always been so different from the rest of my family, almost as if I were the black sheep. I've always viewed things differently and interpreted situations more intensely than the rest. I mean, here I am creating a whole storyline about what happened with the car and the time frame that Dillon was away when no one else is paying any mind to it and just taking it as it is. But my mind won't let me do that.

If someone asked me what I think happened, I'd tell them that Dillon and Damien were planning this for some time. That they knew they were going to make their move when Mom and I went away for the weekend, that Dillon grabbed his passport knowing they weren't going to be coming back. I would say that something along the way went wrong, whether it involved drugs, money, or both and that a situation which they hadn't planned for unraveled in the spur of a moment when something didn't go their way. Maybe someone "wronged" them and that person ended up paying the price, leaving Dillon and Damien no choice but to dump the car off somewhere when their attempts to clean the Escape failed. And I know Dillon— he's extremely intelligent. He knew they fucked up and that he had to act quickly to create a story to save his ass if questions were raised. I think he jumped onto Facetime with Jennifer the second they got back to the apartment, or someplace quiet and acted like he didn't know where Damien was to set the stage. Damien could have been in the next room for all I know. I think Dillon then sent those messages to Damien to try to strengthen said alibi. I think Dillon was anxious and on edge and that's why those messages seemed so odd and out of place. Maybe Damien had enough of it, and responded in the way that he did to make it sound like bullshit. Because it is bullshit. It wouldn't surprise me if Dillon was sitting right next to him as he was sending those. Damien's message was sent the night before Dad got the message to come pick him up. A fight probably broke out between the two of them over that situation and that's why Dillon wanted to leave and in such a hurry! That's why he didn't want Dad talking to Damien or finding out where the car was. That's why Dillon planted the seed of there being blood in the car in the first place to make it seem like he wasn't involved in it from the very start. And now that he's had time to come down from that rush, think clearly, and feel that what he and Damien share is true love, he's going to play stupid and act like he has no knowledge about the car. He's trying to save both himself, and Damien now.

I'll never tell anyone my theory though. No one is going to care anyway. Dad likes to act as if nothing is happening, as if everything is always fine and Mom just forgives and forgets. She'll get angry initially; she'll claim things need to change, then she calms down. She gets over it. She loses that energy and spark and just returns back to her normalcy. She'll scream and curse at you one minute, then an hour or so later she'll ask you what you want for dinner like everything that had happened prior got erased. It's as if it never took place to begin with. Now that I think about it, that takes a mental toll. I never learned how to express myself. I learned that when something goes wrong to just keep to myself because it wouldn't make a difference anyway. There was never any conversations or resolutions to situations that took place growing up, only yelling and threats followed by something desirable later on. That cycle repeated itself my entire life. I'm sure once I get back home that Mom will ask me where I want her to order dinner from and we'll continue on just like that.

Maybe that cycle which Dillon and I grew so accustomed to affected him differently. He's always been the outspoken one. He's the type that always needed to express his feelings, to gain a deeper understanding of a situation and people's intentions and that was never given to him. He was never given explanations or apologies. I'm sure he internalized things that were said to him and took it to heart without anyone ever knowing. This is what he learned to do. To react then move on as if nothing was wrong. And just like that, things started to make sense. Things began to click on in my head. He learned this from Mom. Not to this extent, of course; there's clearly a mental health issue in the mix but he's just doing what we were taught. That's why he's so confused right now about what's going on. He was taught that no matter what was done or said that everything would revert back to normal after his emotions died down. And this is exactly what Mom is doing right now.

CHAPTER 29:
FLIPPING THE SCRIPT

Surprisingly enough, over the next two days, the chaos began to disintegrate. Outsiders were slowly losing interest as Dillon wasn't around to fuel the fire for all to see, which I was thankful for. This shouldn't have been made into a show for entertainment purposes in the first place, but what's done is done. I couldn't shake the eerie feeling though that would flood my chest each time I looked out from my window and saw the Escape lurking in the shade from the oak tree that overhung the driveway. It was sort of ironic if you think about it. The car was an "Escape," but it made me feel so stuck knowing what lingered within. The story that it told, the horrors that it represented. It didn't bring an escape for anyone. I wanted it gone, but Mom was unsure of what to do with it. She no longer believed it was blood and I stopped caring to even put up that fight with her. Sometimes in life you have to learn to pick your battles, and that wasn't one. I wasn't going to change her mind. I knew better than to try anymore, but I couldn't handle seeing his car taunting me every time I stepped outside. I needed it gone.

I picked up my phone and sent Mom a text. I know I could have walked the few feet it was from my room to hers to try to have a conversation about it, but I found texting to be easier. There's a sort of "buffer" when it comes to texting. It allows you time to process what was said and to think about your response before sending as
opposed to face-to-face interactions which I find to be more stressful from the demanding pressure.

Me: Not trying to start an argument, but can we please figure out
what to do with the car? I know you have your own feelings

I wasn't too sure of which type of response I was going to get back . . . or even if I was going to get one at all. When it came to Dillon, she was always protective of him and if she took my message the wrong way, it could easily set her off again. I wasn't intending to cause problems, but she didn't care to understand the toll that everything was taking on me and, of course, I knew it wasn't only me being affected. We all were. I'm not saying this wasn't traumatic for her. I know it was and I'm aware that everyone processes trauma in their own way. I just felt like the only thing that mattered to her in that moment was how Dillon was going to come out of this and playing damage control on his reputation. I felt like I was the one who was being a nuisance to her and as if she blamed me in a way for how this situation had blown up. I knew that Mom would have probably caved into him at the very beginning and just let him run amuck doing whatever he wanted until he settled down again. But I'm sure she's going to pin this on me somehow, claiming I was the "unreasonable" one making something out of nothing when she's the one making nothing out of something!

But to my shock, I didn't get a nasty text response. Instead it read: "I called your father. He is going to clean it and take it for detailing." I didn't answer as I was still cautious of the situation and wasn't sure if something else would follow. Sometimes Mom would give into something that you wanted to make it seem like she was listening to you and heard your point of view just to hold it over your head and use it as ammunition to get something out of it. She always seemed to ask you to do something that you didn't really want to do then threaten to pull back what she had agreed to earlier. I was sure it was only a matter of time before this was thrown in my face as well.

About an hour later, Mom sent me another text asking if I could place the keys to the Escape into the mailbox as Dad was going to come pick it up but wasn't able to hang around. A knot tied in my chest just from thinking about touching the key. A key that could very well have been from a gruesome murder. I know that probably seems over the top and theatrical—*it's just a key*—but my mind couldn't stop. Each moment that went by, my thoughts intensified about the terrors that could have taken place. I couldn't shut my brain off; I couldn't make it stop. I didn't want to touch the key. I didn't want to look outside. I didn't want to see the image of the crimson splattered and absorbed into the seats every time I closed my eyes. My breaths began to multiply as the time between my inhales and exhales shortened. I lay in my bed thinking of the key, terrified to touch it. My fists clenched as I pushed a pillow into my face trying to calm my breathing. If I told Mom I didn't want to touch the key, she would huff and puff and tell me to knock it the fuck off. She'd tell me to grow up and to get over myself, but I wasn't doing this on purpose. I couldn't help it. I was losing control.

My phone vibrated and it was another text from Mom. "If you're not going to answer me then I'll tell him to forget it." I wanted to scream! She has no idea what I'm struggling with. She thinks I'm just going on about my day actively ignoring her without a care in the world. But even if she did know, it wouldn't change anything. I managed to sit up as my head spun looking at the phone screen. I began holding my breath and exhaling slowly to calm myself down. "Sorry, thought I answered. Doing it now." I sent. I know she knew that was a lie, but it was better than telling her I was having a meltdown over a damn car key.

I took one last deep breath in and released it as I stood up from my bed and made my way to the hallway and down the stairs, stopping on the last one. I stood there for a moment staring at the key hooks on the wall by the door. Then I went for it. *Just get it over with,* I thought. I walked towards the key dangling quietly from the hook, gripped it with my right hand as my left turned the knob to the front door to open and tossed the key into the metal mailbox that hung from the house outside of the entry way. I felt an instant relief as I heard it clunk onto the bottom of the box. *Please be over now*, I prayed to myself as I stepped back inside and closed the door, slowly turning the lock. As if that would keep this all from returning.

Later on that day, Mom came downstairs and assisted herself into the living room onto the sofa across from me where I was slumped on the couch with my knees to my chest, playing on my phone. I didn't bother looking up from the screen. *Please don't talk to me; please don't talk to me; please don't talk to me,* I repeated over and over again in my head. I didn't want to engage. I just wanted to be left alone.

But sure enough, Mom didn't pick up on that. "I just got off the phone with your father," she said, breaking the silence.

I took a second to respond. I raised my eyes over my phone to look at her then back down. "Mhm," I answered. I was waiting for her to say something about the car, maybe Dad found something or was calling to say he couldn't clean it. That wouldn't shock me, blood's a bitch to get out to begin with.

"The hospital called. They're planning on releasing Dillon Thursday," she spoke in a calm tone. It seemed like she was almost excited about it but was trying to hide it to wait for a reaction. I mean, why wouldn't she be excited? Her pride and joy did it. He really fooled everyone, including professionals and that only took a few days. That's something every parent should be proud about.

I let out a slight chuckle before answering, "Congratulations."

Mom's eyes got dark and focused on me. I could feel her stare closing in. I continued to play on my phone, avoiding eye contact, waiting for the screaming match to break out. But it didn't. "Can you stop with this already? He's your brother." Her voice took an annoyed pitch, but she wasn't screaming. Usually sarcastic remarks like that would have sent her over the edge. She wanted something. I just wasn't sure what. Then it clicked. I sprung up from the couch, almost tripping over Hershey, and panic kicked in. "He's not coming here," I sternly stated as the tightness in my chest returned.

Mom looked more annoyed now than a minute ago. It was like she was angry that I picked up on her game and beat her to the punch line. "What else do you want, Riley?" She began to yell: "He's fine! You wanted him to get help and he did! He's fine!"

I couldn't believe she had really convinced herself that he was fine. If someone told me I was living in the twilight zone, I would have believed them. "He's not fine!" I screamed back with a crack in my voice. "He played everyone! We're all part of his fucking merry-go-round! Its barely been a week, do you seriously think he got the help he needs in that time?! It's a fucking game and he won!" I continued.

"Jesus Christ almighty! They wouldn't release him if he wasn't okay!" Mom belted.

In that moment, everything went black. I had so much anger, I was becoming convinced that I was the crazy one. That I was making this all up in my head because how could everyone around me be so blind to what was happening? I'm pretty sure my soul left my body at that point in time because I could see myself standing there. I was looking at myself from the corner of the room. I saw my veins bursting through my arms as I was gripping the top of my head with both hands looking Mom dead in the eyes. I couldn't even focus on how to respond or what to say. There were hundreds of words blasting through my head and with each thought my chest grew tighter and tighter. I had to leave the situation. I watched myself storm up the stairs to my room as Mom continued yelling. I'm not even sure what she was saying at that point.

"He's not coming here!" I blurted as I reached the top of the stairs.

"If your ass would have listened and let me speak instead of being so fucking thick-skulled, you would have known that we decided he was going to stay with your father to give things a chance to settle down, but you fucking know everything, right?!" Mom snipped back all in one breath as I slammed the door to my room as hard as I could. I felt the walls shake while my sports trophies fell from the shelves, shattering onto the ground. I put my back up against the door and slid down, crouched on the floor.

He really did it. He really won. He's going to get away with it. With all of it. Everything he did is going to get swept under the rug and forgotten about. Mom and Dad are just going to move on and go on with their lives like none of this ever happened. Are they fucking kidding me? When does this end?! What was all of this for? Are they actually convinced that hospitals don't release patients unless they're completely fine? C'mon. Especially with mental health, it's not a snap of a finger cure. They probably diagnosed him and set him up with a plan which they expect him to follow, but we all know he isn't going to follow it. He's telling Dad that he's fine and they're both believing him! I know damn well that the hospital/doctors didn't call them themselves. Dillon's not a minor, they aren't going to call "Mommy and Daddy" to tell them that their son's all packed and ready to go! Mom thinks I'm an idiot if she truly thought I was going to believe that the "hospital" called. They're not even on his HIPAA. They can't even disclose anything to begin with. Does she really think I'm that stupid? And how's he going to be when he gets out?! Angry? Revengeful? Proud of himself? He fucking did it. He really did it.

I stayed in my room slumped on the floor against the door for the rest of the day. My body was too numb to move, and I felt safe there. Back against the door knowing it couldn't be opened. Nothing could come in. I was safe. Hours must have passed when the tears finally dried. The pressure in my chest remained but I felt calm. Or maybe that was just exhaustion. I heard Mom making her way up the stairs as she was clearly talking on the phone. I held my breath as she came closer to my door, making sure I didn't make a sound. I didn't want her to know that I was up. I couldn't take any more fighting. "Even if he does speak to me he's going to have to stay with you; your daughter thinks she's a fucking princess. It's hell with her here, Pete, fucking hell. She's going to drive me into my grave," Mom spoke extra loudly into the phone as she passed my room, making sure that I could hear. She always knew how to take jabs to fuck with one's head. She's always flipping the script. I'm not sure why I thought this time would be any different. Now it's my fault. I wanted to bang my head against the door out of frustration, but I couldn't give her that satisfaction. I wanted to go back at her, but I couldn't do that either. Giving any kind of reaction to her only makes her feel accomplished. That's one thing I've come to learn throughout the years; she enjoys knowing that she got to you. That she got under your skin. But dammit; does it get to my fucking head!

I'm the problem? Is she fucking kidding me? What did I do? What did I fucking do? Why can't I ever just talk to her? Why is it always a fight? Why does she always manipulate the situation to make it seem like I'm this horrible person? Does she just hate me or am I really such a problem to everyone? Why does she get so mean? Why does she always hold Dillon up on a pedestal? He literally stole thousands of dollars from her! He told her he was going to slice her throat like a fucking pig and burn her to crumbs, but I'm the problem? I'm the one driving her to her grave? I'm the one making it hell? I don't want to be here anymore. I can't take it anymore. I'm so tired, I'm so fucking tired. Where do I tap out? Where's the stop button? Please, someone, just get me out of here. Get me FUCKING out of here!

CHAPTER 30:
DILLON'S RETURN

Thursday came. Mom and I were still not speaking which was probably for the best. She so kindly made sure to keep me in the loop of things by loudly speaking every time she was on the phone, making sure I heard. I knew she wanted a reaction from me, but I didn't give her one. I acted as if I either didn't hear her or that I simply didn't care. I think I did a pretty good job at it, considering she repeated, "I turned his phone back on and it'll be in the mailbox for you to pick up on your way to get him" twice." Once while she was coming down the stairs as I was laid out on the couch watching videos on my phone, then again word for word seconds later, only slightly louder, as she was now standing directly in the entrance to the room. She stopped her walker dead center and made it look as if she couldn't speak into the phone and walk at the same time, but I knew she was putting on a spiteful act. I gave no reaction, no expression, not even an eye roll. I wasn't giving her the satisfaction or playing into the mind games.

You know what? Come to think of it, I'm not sure if Mom even knew what she wanted to do considering how she kept going back and forth between putting her foot down and giving in. The day prior, she seemed pretty stern on the phone with Dad regarding the car. Dad was able to clean it; don't ask me how, but kept pushing Mom on the idea of giving it back to Dillon when he got out. At first Mom was adamant on selling it. She wanted some type of reimbursement for everything that she lost. For once, I was actually proud of her for what seemed like discipline and consequences for Dillon. I mean, why *should* he get it back? After all the hell he put her through and how he walked over her as if she were nothing but chewed gum stuck onto the pavement of a sidewalk? Who is he to get a single thing from her? But, of course, Dad started with his "superhero" act trying to save the day. He began with comments such as "C'mon, Rita, the kid is going to need a car", "How is he going to get around?", "Don't you want him to get a job?", and my favorite, "Hasn't he been through enough?"

I'm sorry. "Hasn't he been through enough?" What the fuck kind of mockery is that?! Hasn't Mom been through enough? Haven't I been through enough? Hasn't our family been through enough? How in the world is he being turned into some kind of victim in all of this? All of this happened BECAUSE of him! HE did this! But HE'S been through enough? This has got to be some kind of fucking joke.

By the end of the conversation, Mom had obviously caved in and was on the same page as Dad about giving the car back. In fact, she seemed excited about it as if it were her idea from the start and like it was going to be such a good thing for him. Like Dillon deserved it. I couldn't do anything but roll my eyes as I heard the conversation unfold. Stupid me keeps hope alive that something is going to change, but I guess I don't learn from my mistakes either. Maybe Dillon and I have more in common than I thought. Anyway, it was sort of comical in a sense how Mom's now walking around trying to throw it in my face that he's not only getting his car back but his phone too. Why does she even want to throw anything at me to begin with? What's the point of all of this? If getting me emotionally worked up makes her happy or makes her feel like she's in control of something in life, then so be it. I'm done with these games.

But wait, that's it. Maybe Mom picks at me like this to make her feel in control of something. She takes her helplessness about Dillon and flings it onto me to make her feel like she's in charge. Like she actually still has a say over how things go and has power over me. It makes her feel good about herself. But why? Why is she so restrained with Dillon? I get being scared and not wanting to deal with things but why eat at me? Why put a strain on our relationship for no reason? I've already grown up feeling as I don't belong, like I'm second best. I worked my ass off in school. I followed all the rules—everything to make her proud. To get her approval. But it never lasts. Maybe she genuinely just doesn't like me. Maybe she blames me for Shane. If I hadn't gotten sick, we would have been home that day. That tragedy may have never happened. Everything might have been so different. Maybe we would have been one big happy family. Ugh, stop it. Stop it, Riley. You can't think like that. It's not your fault. It's not my fault.

Later that night I received a video message from Dillon on SocialFriends. A pit engulfed my chest. I was positive it was going to be of him angry, seeing that I had accessed his accounts. Surely he had put two and two together when he got to Dad's and tried to log onto his things only to find that his password had been changed along with the several messages stating the requested change. He had to have known it was me; neither Mom nor Dad are technology savvy. I guess I didn't think this far ahead when I was doing it. I never thought of the outcome or what would follow. I couldn't blame him though for being mad when I essentially invaded such personal things. I know I would be absolutely furious if roles were switched.

I lingered my finger over my phone screen, hesitant to press "play" on the video. I wasn't ready for it. I wasn't in the mood to entertain him or this any longer, but I just wanted to get it over with. I reluctantly tapped my screen to start the video. I guess either he didn't piece things together or he just didn't care because he wasn't mad. He made no mention of what I had done but, instead, it was a video of him jumping up and down on the twin-sized mattress in Dad's spare bedroom at his house. There was a Little Mermaid comforter set made on the bed as that spare room was used for Kathy's granddaughter, Ashlee, who was three years old. I watched Dillon bounce up and down repeatedly on the bed as Ariel's face would scrunch beneath his feet. He had such a gleaming smile stretched across his face of excitement reminding me of a child on vacation jumping on their hotel room bed. "He-he-he-ahhh," he playfully yelled in between jumps. "I'm back, I'm back, baby Ashlee," he repeated over and over again as he picked up speed on his jumps. "Baby Ashlee, baby Ashlee, baby Ashlee;" his eyes grew bigger as he let out more giggles and playful screams. "Vagina, vagina, vagina, vagina, vagina, he-he-he, ha-ha-ha, ho-ho-ho," he continued.

I wasn't too sure what to make of the video. It's like nothing the last two weeks even happened. He seemed so unaffected by it all. He was truly untouchable. That's when I realized that maybe he did piece together the puzzle that I was the one behind accessing his accounts. This video could have served as a "fuck you" message to me, showing me that nothing is going to end this, that he's still carrying on and that there's nothing I could do to stop him. That eerie feeling in my gut returned. He was onto me. I clicked on his profile to see if anything new had been posted to find that he had removed me as a friend. *Oh, he definitely knows*, I thought to myself. Although he had deleted me as a friend, his profile wasn't private which meant I could still view his posts. There was a new post that had shown to be posted about fifty minutes prior which read:

Dillon Venturi: Hello all. I am back from my vacation. Yes, I did say vacation because that's what it was. I'm sure many of you will hold your opinions on a psychological institution based off of the unfortunate stereotype and negative stigma that it holds, but I am here to assure you that none of it is true. In fact, I highly recommend everyone to gain the experience of a lifetime. I had my own room; there were fridges and pantries stocked at all hours of the day with anything of your choosing. Huge, flat-screen televisions, and many leisurely activities. The best part? It was all FREE. That's right, a free vacation. What more could you ask for? I also came across many good-hearted people who society just didn't seem to understand. I made many friends who I look forward to keeping in touch with and I am overly excited to make my return in the future. And for anyone wondering, I am clinically well; any and all claims of my "insanity" fabricated by my family have been unfounded. - Xoxo, Dillon – *Posted 9:06pm*

Of course, why would I expect anything else? I said to myself as I continued to scroll his page, clicking onto the comment section where, of course, there were people congratulating him and wishing him the best of luck. I sat there and rolled my eyes at the stupidity. I clicked off the post and scrolled further down his page. I was planning on checking the comments on the older posts to see if anything recent was said since I had last checked when a post from Archer caught my eye. It was posted three days before Dillon had gone in for the psychiatric evaluation. I must have missed it in all of the chaos; it was difficult to keep up with.

Archer LaCoco: I think you've been eclipsed! The lunar eclipse fell in your twelfth house of craziness — *Posted 17 days ago*
Dillon Venturi: Did it? What does that mean? — *Posted 17 days ago*
Archer LaCoco: It explains your family wanting to commit you to a psych ward. Twelfth house rules over that. The eclipses this month are activating your health houses. — *Posted 17 days ago*
Dillon Venturi: I am as healthy as a goat — *Posted 17 days ago*
Archer LaCoco: This eclipse's effects last for around a year or so. It doesn't happen right away — *Posted 17 days ago*
Dillon Venturi: Stop it — *Posted 17 days ago*
Dillon Venturi: You stop it right now — *Posted 17 days ago*
Dillon Venturi: You take that back — *Posted 17 days ago*
Dillon Venturi: I will not have this behavior — *Posted 17 days ago*
Archer LaCoco: Unfortunately I do predict some mental health issues coming. The lunar eclipse conjuncted your North Node in the twelfth house while it squared your Pluto, ruler of psychology — *Posted 17 days ago*

I had no idea what any of that meant. I tried googling it to get a better understanding of the astrology terminology, but that just made things even more confusing. Results stated something about the twelfth house having to do with your subconscious, though I don't know what the twelfth house even means to begin with. I lightly laughed to myself after reading that post; maybe Archer really wasn't a fraud after all, since he foreshadowed the events that were just days away. Or maybe he came to the realization that Dillon was off his rocker like all of us and stated the inevitable. It's funny, after that post Archer made no more comments on any of Dillon's things and when I clicked on his name to view his profile it no longer showed Dillon as a friend. I *wonder* what happened there.

CHAPTER 31:
JUST A DREAM?

It took two extra days of tiptoeing around one another for Mom to finally speak to me, which turned into a disaster. *What a surprise.* She calmly knocked twice on my bedroom door, "Riley?" she spoke.

I was slouched on my bed with my knees up watching music videos on my phone. I looked up towards the door and held my breath, hesitant to answer. The heaviness in my chest returned immediately. I knew it wasn't going to be good. Mom wouldn't come to me after all of this so quickly to make amends. "Yeah?" I regretfully replied.

Mom opened the door and walked in positioning her walker against my desk as she took a seat, facing my direction. The silence of our stare felt like forever as I lightly giggled due to nerves. "Can I help you?" I laughed.

"I just want to talk," Mom answered. "Dillon is coming over later today; he's ready to talk and I would like for you to be there," she continued. I shook my head and looked back down toward my phone. I told her I had no desire to see or speak to him.

"Fuck it, Riley. Can you stop your bullshit already?" she sniped back.

"No, I'm not going to stop it. I'm not burying this all under the rug like you and Dad are. He's not okay and you guys refuse to see it!" I yelled.

"Why can't you see that he's better? He's doing so well!" Mom raised her voice back.

I was dumbfounded. *Did she really just try telling me that he's magically better?*

"He's better? All of a sudden, he's better? All those years of being addicted to drugs and he's better within days? His anger and behavior since a child is magically gone overnight?"

"Jesus Christ, he wasn't an addict, Riley. He was a user!" Mom yelled.

I had no words. She was completely brainwashed. There was no way he was that good at manipulating. There was just no way. I don't think Mom believed herself either. I think she was just spitting out whatever came to mind to try to convince me and maybe even convince herself that that was true. But I wasn't buying it. Someone doesn't go from shooting up daily over the course of several years to just blinking and being done with it. Especially something such as crystal meth. I'm not dumb; he's not done with it and I refuse to fall back into this trap. If Mom wants to, then so be it but until he admits he has a problem and seeks the help that he so desperately needs, I can't have him back into my life. I can't go through this again which is what I told her. Mom didn't seem to understand though, but that shouldn't have been a shock. She just became angrier, screaming about how selfish I was and how I needed to recognize when Dillon was doing well and give him the credit that he apparently deserved.

Honestly, it was hard not to crack a smile while she was yelling. I couldn't take her seriously. *Give him credit? Credit for what? Fooling everyone? Yeah, sure, good job, Dillon. I'm so very proud of you.* I was waiting for someone to burst through the door telling me that this was a joke—it had to be. I couldn't make sense of this otherwise. I felt like telling Mom and even Dad that they should go and educate themselves on drug addiction at the very least. Like forget about the mental health aspect here for a second, just the drug issue alone in itself should be enough to make Mom and Dad pause to recognize the true extent of addiction. It doesn't take a rocket scientist to understand addiction and the severity, especially when it comes to someone who doesn't admit that there's even a problem to begin with. Addiction alone is a lifelong battle— throw untreated mental illness into the mix and you've got yourself an explosion waiting to happen, but Mom and Dad weren't ready for that conversation, and I doubted at that point that they would ever be.

It was just shy of 2:30 when the gravel stones began to shuffle under the weight of tires pulling into the driveway. I peeked from my window blinds and instantly felt my chest begin to enclose. There it was. The black Escape. The darkness it held. *It's back. It's all back, isn't it?*

Mom was already sitting on the porch, waiting, "Hi baby," she called out as Dillon was getting out from the car. His appearance looked well; I'll give him that. His facial hair was neatly buzzed, he had on a navy collared shirt, similar to a Polo and lightly faded jeans with a designer rip at the knee. I'm guessing Dad took him shopping because the clothing that he had bagged up when he came to clear out Dillon's room was stained, mixed with trash, needles, and whatever other junk was piled in there. Or maybe Dillon and Damien went on a shopping spree with all of the things they stole from Mom, but that can't be it. All Dillon had when Dad picked him up was a small backpack. I doubted he had fit much in it. And that would be just like Dad. Taking him out to get pampered. To get rewarded for his behavior. It probably made Dad feel like the big guy, like he was stepping up and helping him; meanwhile, Dillon most likely viewed it as an accomplishment. He loved having Dad and pretty much anyone right where he wanted them. Wrapped around his finger.

Aside from his appearance he seemed nervous in his gait. Hesitant while walking towards the porch but instantly snapped into character once he came into view of Mom, flashing that charming smile that we've grown to know so well. "How are you, baby?" Mom asked as he approached the steps. I had to move away from the window. My chest became too heavy to handle as I sat on the bed cupping my face into a pillow trying to shallow my breaths. Images of the blood-stained seats flashed through my head along with everything else that's happened the last few weeks. My thoughts were screaming. My fingers began to dig through the pillow into my face, squeezing tighter with each flashed memory. My teeth clenched tightly. I needed everything to stop. I needed my mind to turn off, but it got louder instead. Suddenly I heard the front door swing open and familiar footsteps drag in. My heart stopped but raced at the same time.

I sat, frozen and quiet on the bed, attentively tracking the sound of his steps. I was anticipating the creaks of the stairs to echo through the hall as he made his way up just like in my dreams. Lately, when I managed to fall asleep there's been a recurring theme that happens; I'm asleep in my bed when I'm awoken by the front door pushing open and the sound of weighted steps gently creaking their way up the staircase, stopping in front of my bedroom door. The door flings open and it's Dillon standing in the entrance way with a blank stare through his eyes. I say nothing. I try to move, but go nowhere. The blankets become weighted like chains holding me in place. "I'm sorry I have to do this, but I can't live like this anymore," Dillon mockingly speaks as he steps into the room towards the bed, pulling a syringe out from his back pocket. Just as he approaches the bed, Mom walks by and looks in. Dillon begins to laugh, puts the syringe back into his pocket and walks out towards Mom as they both laugh together down the hall.

Now that I think of it, this dream wasn't fully just a dream. Back in 2010, I was in my room watching tv from my bed when I heard Dillon coming up the stairs. My door was wide open as he walked directly in and closed the door behind him. He had a sly smirk across his face. "Stay seated," he softly spoke. I looked down and he was holding one of Mom's insulin needles in his hand. I asked him what he was doing, and he said "I'm sorry I have to do this, but I just can't live like this anymore." He lifted the needle up towards me, holding it as if it were a knife.

Mom walked through the door seconds later. "Dillon, what are you doing? I told you I needed to take my insulin."

Dillon instantly started to laugh as he turned to Mom. "I was just messing with her; here you go," he said, handing

Mom the needle. Mom looked at him and for a second I thought she was going to question him further but then she cracked a smile, "You're so fucked up." She laughed it off as she made her way out of my room and back to hers. Dillon turned back towards me to flash his charm and shrug his shoulders in an "oh, well" motion before also walking out of my room, closing the door behind him.

In that moment though, I wasn't fearful either, so I don't blame Mom for laughing it off. It was just Dillon messing around as usual. I mean, that's what we all thought back then anyway. But now? Now I don't know what to think. Clearly, that's where this dream is stemming from—only now it's a real fear. I didn't think anything of it back then, but now my brain is running in circles trying to make sense of it. *Was he trying to kill me back then? Was he actually being serious? What would have happened if Mom didn't walk in?* Honestly though, Mom probably would have reacted in the same sense. Laughing it off. Making a joke of it, flipping it around to make it seem like it was me. *Why would I expect differently?* She's showed me time and time again that she'll choose him. She'll favor him. I can see it so clearly; she'd walk in and start yelling at him. Asking him what the fuck is wrong with him, talking a big game. Then, he'd go at her and she'd back down. She'd apologize to him and make it my fault. My fault for him trying to kill me. I wouldn't be surprised if she helped him cover it up either. So this dream isn't really farfetched if you think about it.

The echoes never buzzed up the stairs; instead, Dillon's footsteps softened as they made their way through the front of the house and into the kitchen. I remained frozen. I was waiting for him to come up the stairs; my heart was pounding so fast it felt as if it was going to break through my ribs and tear through my skin. About five minutes went by when the footsteps began to louden towards the front of the house. I held my breath. The front door opened and then swung shut. "All right, Mommy, I should get going now," Dillon's voice flew through the air and into my open window.

"Okay, baby, thank you for coming. Get back safe," Mom replied with disappointment. One would think that Dillon leaving would start to soothe my mind but instead everything amplified as I listened for the tires leaving the driveway. I gasped for air as I broke down in tears, falling to the floor. I couldn't help but sob.

CHAPTER 32:
OF COURSE, A COVER UP

It was close to noon when Hershey jetted to the door barking, alerting that someone was there. I peeked out of the living room window to see a police cruiser stationed in the driveway. *Just give me a fucking break,* I thought to myself. I was still numb from Dillon's visit the day before and my soul had nothing left in me. I took a deep breath in and called up for Mom. "The cops are here."

I answered the door as Officer Phillips stood a few feet back with a manilla folder tucked in his hand. "Hello ma'am, is Rita here?"

Just as I was about to answer, Mom came up behind me. "Yes, officer?" she questioned.

Officer Phillips glanced down at the folder before looking back up at Mom and answering, "Yes, good afternoon ma'am. I'm here following up on a report back from August regarding your son. Do you have a moment to talk?"

Mom motioned for the officer to come in and told him they could speak in the kitchen as Officer Phillips followed. Obviously I wanted to eavesdrop, but going into the kitchen with them would be all too obvious and considering Mom and I still weren't on the best of terms, I quietly stayed in the living room. It was close enough to hear the conversation but far enough not to draw attention. Mom offered him a cup of coffee in which he politely declined as I heard the crinkles of paper turning. I assumed he had opened the folder.

"So the last we spoke, you, uh, had some concerns of your son with the taking of your car and some threats," Officer Phillips spoke attentively.

"Yes, I've been meaning to call. We got it all sorted and I actually wanted to drop the charges," Mom answered softly.

"Drop the charges?" Officer Phillips questioned with a concerned tone.

"Yes, um, we were able to locate him, and he voluntarily went in for a psychological evaluation. He's doing well and that's all I wanted. I no longer wish to press charges," Mom responded.

"Okay. Uh, well, we can drop the car charges—no problem. You'd just have to sign off on that but, unfortunately, when it comes to domestic violence and threats such as those that your son was sending, you aren't able to drop those specific ones."

There was a slight stillness before Mom cautiously answered: "What? What do you mean? I don't want to press charges on him; he had a meltdown which he's receiving help for. I don't—"

"I understand. Unfortunately, that is out of even my control. When it comes to domestic cases such as these, it's strictly up to the courts and the DA on proceeding. You'd be more than welcome to plead that with the judges and express your wishes and such," Officer Phillips interrupted.

There was another thin pause. I could tell Mom was considering what to do next. There's no way she was going to back down that easily but at the same time . . . how was she going to wiggle her way out of the law? For a quick moment, I had excitement that life finally caught up to Dillon, that he was finally going to be held accountable, and that it was out of Mom's and Dad's hands to put any end to it. I should have known better though because that's not how this story goes. There wasn't going to be any justice or any reality checks for him because the next thing I knew, Mom uttered, "What if it wasn't Dillon?"

I'm sure that statement threw Officer Phillips off just as much as it did me because he took a moment to respond, and when he did, he seemed hesitant and stuttered among his words. "Was it, was it not him?" Officer Phillips asked.

"It wasn't Dillon. It turns out the guy he was with, Damien Reyes, had taken a hold of his phone and was the one sending the messages. Dillon had no idea what was happening. He would never say such things." Mom lied through her teeth. I know the officer knew she was lying but what could he do? There was no proof saying otherwise. He simply explained to Mom that she would have to write a statement that would be submitted to the DA and hopefully that would rid Dillon of the current charges which she gladly wrote, signed, and Officer Phillips was out the door as swiftly as that.

Even though I wasn't surprised, I was infuriated. Mom lying on legal documentation took this game to a whole new level. This coverup was absolutely ridiculous and even the officer knew it. But this was the way it went.

At what cost is enough, enough? What's going to happen when it's discovered that what she wrote is a bunch of bullshit? When does it end? When will someone step the fuck up and stop covering up for him? Everywhere I turn someone is shielding him, making excuses for him, putting themselves on the line to avoid him having repercussions. When is enough, enough?!

CHAPTER 33:
AN UNAMUSED WARNING

Four months had passed with things settling down, almost as if none of it ever happened. Dillon and Mom were on great terms again; no one knew of any diagnosis. Dillon claimed he was fine, and Mom and Dad gullibly believed it. But that's no shocker, *right?*

As for me, my anxiety grew uncontrollably to the point of daily panic attacks, especially the days when Dillon would come over. I had to leave the house each and every time beforehand and couldn't come back until he was gone. And when I would come back? I had to inspect everything. I was constantly in fight or flight mode. I made sure every window, every door, every access point was locked. I made sure if any drinks were opened in the fridge that they were tossed. Same with any opened food, I refused to touch it unless I personally opened it right then and there. I didn't trust him. I didn't trust him one bit. I was terrified he was going to send someone in the middle of the night for me, or that he was going to do something to my drinks or food like Mom had suspected all that time ago. Even my shampoo bottles and toothbrush I kept locked in my room. I was the paranoid one now. Mom constantly pushed down my throat how ridiculous and dramatic I was being. As if I was doing it on purpose. But I couldn't handle it. Just the thought of Dillon sent my heart racing. The blood. I couldn't get the blood out of my head, and he drove that car around without a care in the world. And I was so very tired of Mom and me fighting over him and putting a wedge between us. "He's fine. He's got a job; he's doing so much better. Can't you see that? Can't you stop your shit already and forgive him?" Mom would say. I stopped trying to plead my case. She never listened anyway.

I tried telling Mom again and again how someone doesn't just stop using the kind of drugs that he was using for all those years with a snap of a finger. I desperately tried to get it through her head that he wasn't okay and that he would cycle again. I would scream and cry and get myself worked up just begging her to look at it rationally. To do something. To get him help. But she wanted to hear none of it. It was easier for her and Dad just to wipe their hands clean of this. Now *I* was the enemy. *I* was the problem. So I kept to myself. Mom would tell me when Dillon was coming over and I'd leave for a few hours until he was gone. Sometimes I was told that he would be spending the night so I would go and get myself a hotel. I didn't mind the hotels to be honest. They would calm me. I didn't have to check everything or live on edge. I could just relax in a safe space. It got to the point where I would tell people that I was the only child, or just refer to Shane. Dillon had no place in my life any longer. I cried, I yelled, I mourned. I went through the entire grief process for someone who was still alive and doing that was so much harder than grieving someone who had actually passed. But I had to do it. I knew this wasn't over and that an explosion would come again. I refused to be a casualty. If he wasn't going to get the help he greatly needed, then I couldn't have a brother named Dillon. I couldn't go through this again.

Though my worries seemed irrational to Mom and Dad, they were all proved true when I woke up to a message on SocialFriends from a Billy Wurkel. I had no idea who he was, I had never even heard of his name before now. I opened the message and began reading: "Dillon Venturi has been giving out information about you and your family including phone numbers, addresses, places of employment and where you go to college." The heaviness in my chest instantly returned along with fear and anxiety.

"I knew he wasn't fucking done!" I shouted as I stormed out of my room, barging into Mom's with adrenaline pumping. I've never seen Mom pop up so quickly out of bed; it was nearing seven in the morning, and I most definitely woke her up in a startle as she flung her arm up in a defensive motion knocking a glass of water and her cell phone off of the side table next to her bed. "You keep dancing around that he's fucking fine and I told you—I told you he wasn't!" I berated her heatedly with my entire chest.

"Wha-what? What the hell are you talking about?" Mom impatiently muttered, still trying to catch her breath and realize her surroundings. My body was shaking with rage and voice cracking as I read the message from the start and continued on: "I'm concerned for the safety of you and your family. He mostly mentions you and your Mom but has also mentioned your father, and a baby Ashlee. He has sent out images and texts of great concern, pornographic and violent. He has been harassing me and my friends online and has been reported. I've been encouraged to contact the authorities and will do so if he doesn't stop texting and calling me."

By now, Mom had settled down and understood what was going on. "Who the hell is this?" she asked, seemingly annoyed.

"I don't know; it doesn't matter," I shot back as I read more of the message aloud.

"I've known Dillon for five years; we met online. The messages are mostly along the lines of things he has sent your mother and father when he is mad or wants attention, but they are ones that I am not comfortable sending you; as I mentioned before, they are pornographic and violent. He continues to send very bloody images. Violent images of women bloody. He is spiraling out of control again and is in need of serious and immediate help."

I looked up from my phone to see how Mom was responding. She sat there, shaking her head and rolling her eyes. I knew this was going to be pointless like everything before but that didn't stop me from reading on. It was like a part of me kept thinking that maybe if I kept going that something would stick with her. "Dillon has also mentioned how angry he is that he cannot come to the house if you are there because of the Damien thing and I am fearful for you and your family's safety. I wanted to do my part to make you aware in case."

"What are you possibly rolling your eyes at?" I yelled.

Mom didn't even hesitate with her answer. "He's full of shit," she responded so confidently. I stood there amazed and not, all at the same time. Her response wasn't a surprise to me at all. I expected this, but I didn't all at once. I know that doesn't make any sense and I wish I had the words to explain it, but I don't.

"Full of shit?" I howled back.

Mom sat there, agitation clearly growing. "Yeah, full of shit, Riley. We don't even know who the hell he is, and you want me to believe that? He's making shit up to stir issues. That's why he won't send you anything that he's claiming! You need to fucking give this act up, Riley. I'm sick of it," Mom firmly stated, struggling to reach down to grab her phone.

I have to give up the act? I'm in the wrong for being worked up over someone reaching out to WARN ME?! What does Dillon actually have to do? Does he have to fucking kill me? Is that it? Will that get Mom's attention? Oh, wait, probably not. Shane- no. Riley, don't even go there. Stop. Stop.

Hopelessness engulfed my lungs as with one last breath, I started to yell back at how careless, reckless, and ridiculous Mom and everyone else has been when it comes to Dillon. There was nothing else I could do but yell.

Mom, of course, interrupted and cut me off. "Enough!" she shouted, putting her hand up in a "stop" gesture. "Just get out of my room, Riley! Leave me alone," she continued as her phone began to ring. "What the hell does your father want now?" she mumbled as she picked up her phone.

CHAPTER 34:
THE GRAND FINALE

I hung my head in defeat and made my way out of Mom's room. I didn't know what I was expecting to come from it anyway. I knew better. But *oh well*. I took a hold of the door knob and began to pull the bedroom door closed behind me.

"Gone? What do you mean gone?" Mom screamed into the phone. I stopped pulling the door closed and stood there with my hand frozen on the knob. Mom looked up at me in fright. "Where the hell would he go?" she questioned. "The car?" she continued.

Just then, my phone in hand buzzed and a text message from Jennifer appeared. I opened the message up to read: "Hey, girl, so sorry to bother you but don't want to worry Mama this early. I woke up to a message from Dillon last night. He wasn't really making sense but said he couldn't stay here and that he had to get out? Then he sent another message that just said Mexico. I tried calling him, but no answer." Once again, my heart dropped to the floor as I made my way back into the room towards Mom, holding out my phone for her to read.

Mom glanced down at my phone, silently reading amongst herself, half listening to what Dad was saying. Her mouth slowly dropped as she cautiously lowered her phone from her ear with fear filling her eyes. Stuttering over her words, but firmly, Mom directed me to "go check the drawer in the kitchen. Now." It took me a moment to process and make sense of what she was asking me to do, then it clicked. My eyes darted open as I rushed downstairs to the kitchen. *No way. No way he fucking took it!* I thought to myself as I yanked open the kitchen drawer to find it empty with nothing but sponges. *Son of a bitch.*

"The passport, Pete. The fucking passport! He took it!" Mom shouted into the phone. "I took it out of the duffle bag when we got back from the hospital and placed it into the drawer. It slipped my mind to put it away. God dammit!" she pleaded. "Jen-Jen said Mexico." I couldn't hear what Dad was saying on the other line, but I assumed he was trying to talk her down so that they could figure out what precisely was going on. All I knew was that Dad woke up this morning to find that Dillon was gone along with an emptied closet and a spare space in the driveway. Who knows where he's actually going. The Mexico text could very well be just another stunt from Dillon to gain a reaction and put the attention back onto him. He doesn't handle it well when the spotlight starts to fade. Both Mom and Dad attempted to call Dillon's line several times with no answer before it started going straight to voicemail without even a single ring.

I began to question if this was his plan all along. If Dillon ever had true intentions of forming peace with Mom or if he instead played the part to get her to put her guard down for one last time so that he could get to what he wanted. So he could find his passport. He clearly knew she took it as it was in his bag when he came here that tiring day for the "intervention" only for it to be gone when he finally got out.

Was he snooping little by little each time he came here? How did he even find that? Or did he just happen to come across it randomly when in need for a sponge? Was this his master plan for a grand finale? Fuck everyone over one last time? His great escape?

Hershey began growling and jumping at the front door as three stern knocks echoed throughout the house. I peeked from the front upper window that was once Dillon's room to find four police cars scattered in the driveway. *What now? What else could be going on?* I looked up to the ceiling and started praying to something that I wasn't sure I even believed in. I'm not sure who I was speaking to, but I kept asking for this to finally end.

"Who is that?" Mom anxiously asked, fearing the answer.

"The police," I gently spoke.

I dreadfully made my way down the stairs with Mom following behind. I waited until her stairlift reached the bottom instead of taking the initiative to answer the door. I didn't want to answer it alone. Honestly, I didn't want to answer it at all. I subtly let Mom take the lead ahead of me as she made her way towards the entrance. The echoes of the knocks grew firmer. I quietly kept my distance as if that was going to protect me from what was to come. Mom glanced back at me, let out a tiresome sigh and turned the knob, pulling the door open.

There stood three officers on the porch with four more in the distance positioned on the front lawn. The leading officer stood about six feet tall with a thick athletic build. He had a freshly shaved scruff beard and remained with his thumbs tucked into the holster belt on either side of his waist. "Good afternoon, ma'am, I'm Officer Ortiz. We're here concerning a vehicle that you reported having with possible blood traces on the seats, which was in the possession of Dillon Venturi and Damien Reyes." Mom stood there stunned, trying her hardest to keep her balance with the walker. "Ye-yes. I had reported that back in August," she nervously uttered.

Officer Ortiz nodded before proceeding. "Understood, ma'am, we're going to need to take another look at the vehicle along with a few questions for, uh, Dillon."

I noticed Mom's weight gradually give out from underneath her. I quickly came up behind, grabbing her hips and assisting her down onto the seat of her walker. Her eyes were the heaviest I've seen. "I was told I could clean the car. The department said it was of no use. I don't . . . I don't have it anymore." Mom's breaths became shallow, trying to hold back from crying.

The officers looked with great concern as Officer Ortiz once again took the lead. "Ma'am, where is the vehicle? Did you sell it? junk it? And how long ago?"

"My, my son has it," Mom softly answered, putting her hand up to her mouth to cover.

"Ma'am, we're investigating a murder with a possible link to that vehicle. Is Dillon Venturi present?" Officer Ortiz followed up, taking his right thumb out from his holster belt, and pressing the side button on his walkie talkie that rested up on his chest attached to his vest before proceeding to speak some coded words into it.

Mom continued to stumble over her words. "That's, that's, that's my son," she helplessly expressed, turning her head to look at me. She was begging for help but there was nothing that I could do. I placed my hand onto her shoulder for comfort.

"Ma'am, is Dillon here?" Officer Ortiz reiterated.

Mom lifted her hand and grabbed onto mine that rested on her shoulder. Tears began to run down her face as she gripped my hand tighter.

"He's . . . he's gone," she answered as distraught, confusion, and reality began to set in.

It was obvious that wasn't the answer Officer Ortiz or any of the officers wanted to hear as a sense of urgency took over. Officer Ortiz became firmer and more impatient as he stepped closer to Mom. The other two officers on the porch turned to signal something towards the four officers stationed on the lawn. I'm not sure what it was but it caused them to tighten their postures as they began to visually scan the yard and their surroundings.

"Do you know where he is? When he'll be back? Who he could be with? When he left? What he was wearing? Any other information other than gone?" Officer Ortiz interrogated her as if Mom was the suspect, which got me angry. I get he was doing his job, trying to get information as quickly as possible, but it was clear Mom was falling apart. Her mind was slowly processing what was taking place, trying to make sense of the situation and instead of showing compassion like giving Mom a few seconds to understand, he stood there berating her in an accusatory tone for not answering as rapidly as he'd like.

Mom hopelessly looked up at me then back towards the officers. Her hand still clinging onto mine that rested on her shoulder, I gripped tighter. Her mouth hesitantly opened, but no words came out. She was completely pale in complexion. "Ma'am," Officer Ortiz pushed further.

"Damien. Damien took the car, he's . . . he's manipulating my son," she faltered, struggling to form words as she gasped for air, tears now flooding her face.

Whatever amount of energy I had left emptied out of my soul as I exhaled slowly, looking down at Mom. *It's never going to end*, I realized. I looked up briefly at the officers with an "I'm-sorry" look before glancing back down. I knew better than to speak up. I knew to keep my mouth shut, because anything I said would be made out as a lie. It would be pointless, and I knew if Mom had to choose between me or Dillon, she would choose Dillon. So I stood in silence.

Officer Ortiz took a deep breath in, shaking his head towards the officers standing beside him as if he knew she was lying, before directing his look back towards Mom.

"Ma'am, Damien Reyes *is* the confirmed deceased."